Tales
of Grief
and
Hope

Catherine Schaff-Stump

MISTRALDOL PRESS

Blairstown, Iowa

Cover Art: Catrina Horsfield
Interior art design: Michele Maakestad

Table of Contents

The Ground is Full of Teeth is biographical. The town of Oscar Springs is really the town where I grew up, and as such, I was able to render its description in painstaking detail. When I sold the story to Paper Golem press, where it was published in Alembical 4, I was asked to consider changing the time frame of the story from the 1970s to current day. I declined, because I needed the educational system in the story to be before Mandatory Reporting Laws.

The incident of child neglect in this story is also based on real life events, although for a change this isn't about my childhood. Rural America was a tough place to grow up for many people. Many people also think I have based Alice on myself, but Alice Brubaker is based on a childhood friend who ultimately went on to college and became an elementary school teacher. She made quite an impact on me, one I didn't know she had until years later.

I'd like to thank Lawrence Schoen and Arthur "Buck" Dorrance for their help in shaping this story. They did some power editing which made this story better.

The Ground is Full of Teeth

Oscar Springs, 1973

Alice reached up the sleeve of her cardigan and pulled out a silk scarf. Random breezes captured her brown hair and flickered it like a candle flame, away from her face, then across her eyes and nose. She secured the scarf under her chin. Squinting, she surveyed the five grades over which she had dominion during the noon hour. She felt a tug at the bottom of her sweater and looked down.

"Junior's bit Mark Halcomb!" Sue Cheevy rang out in the singsong voice of tattletales everywhere.

Alice didn't like Sue, a fat little fourth grader who couldn't mind her own business. She knew that as a teacher, she should try to like all the children, but Sue was the illustration in the dictionary under snitch. Sue's use as a stoolie was hit-and-miss. The informant seemed to relish getting any kid in trouble just to watch the fireworks.

Alice glanced at the girl with Sue, Nora, for confirmation. Nora nodded slowly. Yes, Junior had bitten someone again. Four now, Alice racked up in her head. That was bad news.

Alice blasted her whistle three times, which was the signal for one of the teacher's aides to assume her station. She raced after the girls to the bleachers, conscious of the silence following in her wake. Every student thought they were guilty until the teacher passed them by.

Under the bleachers on his knees, Mark was doubled over, howling, his arm folded in the crease of his waist, blood blooming onto his tan jacket. Alice slid across the bare dirt on her knees, her tights laddering, toward Mark and grabbed his arm. His tears verged on hysteria. The cherry birthmark that crossed his nose and left cheek were purple and the rest of his face was an angry red.

His inner arm was torn open, a half circle of flesh soaked in blood. Sue Cheevy hovered like a vulture. Alice undid the scarf's tight knot under her chin, her bloody fingers slipping. She clamped the scarf over the wound and the boy started, hiccupping tears.

"Sue," said Alice. "Nora. Run to Mrs. Yost. Tell her to bring the nurse."

The girls peeled away from the scene.

"It'll be all right," Alice soothed Mark. "Can you come with me?"

The boy allowed himself to be pulled up, to be led out from under the splintery bleacher boards. A crowd had gathered at the back opening, and it parted like Charlton Heston had told it to. Mark was covered with gore.

"There's Junior!" a random voice from the crowd accused.

Junior imitated the rigid goal post he stood beside. His eyes were hidden behind unkempt hair. A baggy t-shirt blew against the potbelly that spilled over his jeans, not quite covering it. Alice looked away. She had no time for a punitive manhunt now.

Alice's hand vised around Mark's arm. The boy had gone into shock, his eyes unfocused. A children's army marched behind them until they met the nurse, all gauze and caressing concern. The children's army started to follow Mark and the nurse into the building, but they were turned back at the edge of the playground by the on-duty Mrs. Yost.

Alice's sleeve was soaked in blood. She removed the sweater and bundled it, so the offensive sleeve was inside. Shielding her eyes from the sun, she scanned the football field. Sturgeon, the school's principal, had emerged from the backstage door of the auditorium and was guiding Junior toward the main office, thick arms steering Junior's shoulders. As they neared the school, Alice could see the blood on Junior's chin and neck.

She glanced at her wrist. With a fingernail, she scratched dried blood off her watch crystal. Recess was over.

————◆•◆————

Since she didn't have a cigarette, Patrice Smalley fiddled with the pen on Alice's desk like she wanted to take a match to it and set it between her crooked teeth. The cap of the pen skirted her chapped lips several times. Dark shadows under Patrice's eyes were reflected craters from moon shot footage. Patrice tapped the pen on the wooden desk and narrowed her eyes at Alice.

The mother sighed. "I can't make him mind."

"Mrs. Smalley," Alice said, "have you considered Junior might need some professional help?"

The woman shuffled through her purse and pulled a packet of cigarettes out, perching them in the top of the bag. She licked the pen while she did it, swiveling the hard plastic with her tongue like an antenna. "Whatever you people want to do, you do it. I don't see anything making much of a difference."

Alice slid a paper across the desk. "One of the requirements for Junior being allowed to return to school is that he work with a counselor from the Area Education Agency." While Alice rattled off the recommendations about classroom pullouts and working with specialists, she noted Patrice tapping the pen like she was shaking down the tobacco inside. Alice followed Patrice's eyes to the visible Virginia Slims. "If you sign here," Alice said, "we'll get him started."

A scrawl filled the white space above a dotted line. "His daddy ain't gonna like this," she said.

No, Alice thought. He isn't. "Mrs. Smalley," said Alice, "maybe you'd like to talk to someone? The county has services."

Patrice stood up. She jammed the pen in her purse and pulled a filtered cigarette from the package with her lips. "I ain't letting them take my boy away, Miss Brubaker. Child belongs with his mother. If you had children, you'd know that." Patrice sashayed out of the room, one hand groping in her bag for a lighter. She staggered as she tripped over the threshold.

Alice puffed air out of her cheeks and calmed herself down. She glanced down at Patrice's scrawl. At least the school had gotten what it wanted.

The elementary students were gone for the day, although the high schoolers from the third floor lingered. Football season was cranking up. Cheerleading chants echoed from the home economics kitchen. The woodwind-heavy marching band squeaked in the background just within range of hearing. Alice grabbed the discipline contract Patrice signed and a master copy for the autumn leaves coloring sheets.

Her first stop was the office. Erlene waggled her eyebrows in greeting above a phone call. Sturgeon motioned her into his inner sanctum. Alice took the vinyl seat across from the big desk after putting the discipline contract in front of the principal.

He read the document through bifocal lenses. "Bill Halcomb says he's going to take it to law. Good luck, squeezing water out of that turnip."

"Is Mark still in the hospital?"

"Observation. Junior'll be back Monday."

A condescending tilt of his head made Alice feel dismissed. She stood. "I'm not sure about this, putting him back in the regular classroom at all." They'd had this argument three bites ago. Even though they were finally pulling Junior out for sessions, he was still going to have the majority of his classes with regular kids.

"Miss Brubaker," said Sturgeon, "we've covered this."

"I live kitty-corner from his house," Alice repeated in her slow talking-to-an-administrator voice. "That's no place for a kid to live."

"They're poor," said Sturgeon. He flipped the bottom of his striped tie back and forth. "Miss Brubaker, if we took every poor kid out of this school, we wouldn't be teaching any kids."

"Not every poor kid is living in a junkyard," Alice said. She crossed her arms, grasping a bony elbow with each hand. "What will you do if you're wrong? What will you do if he hurts another student?"

Sturgeon sighed, long-suffering, and pinched his nose like a man with a sinus headache. "It's the best we can do. Junior's seeing a counselor like you wanted. You'll be watching him in the classroom, and he won't be playing with the other kids. What could happen?"

All sorts of things, Alice thought as she wandered down the hall into the AV room behind the librarian's desk. Amid projectors and slide machines, she found the mimeograph. She jammed the ditto master into the slot of the metal drum and started cranking. Worksheet after worksheet leafed into the waiting basket, smelling like fresh bread because of the chemicals.

Student gossip would escalate the incident. No teacher or kid would trust Junior again. They shouldn't. Junior needed to be taken out of that home, not go there at the end of the day. He needed to be somewhere where he would have a chance.

The ditto machine stopped when she counted to thirty. She took the damp sheets, straightened them, and returned to her room. The rest of the afternoon vanished in cutting out new desk signs for the students, shaped like autumn leaves. Alice wrote their names carefully: Shelby, Michael E., Michael B., Tim, Abel instead of Junior. She wondered if the new name might help with a new start. It was his father's name, so not likely. She crumpled it and threw it away and wrote Junior on a new leaf.

The afternoon was warm. She left the building, jacket draped over her arm. Two blocks and she was on Main Street. The downtown of Oscar Springs was in various stages of decay. The outside of Luann's had been washed with aqua paint, a color usually reserved for school hallways. The movie theater had a duct-taped repair over the crack in the Plexiglas some young townies had made last Halloween.

Gray buildings, their paint weathered and flaking, hid other stores that were invisible unless you knew they were there. Hopkins Hardware, Key Drug, and Malcott Insurance. The town pride was a vinyl-sided community center, built in 1968, a stenciled sign attributing it to the hardworking people who wanted to make Oscar Springs the brightest spot in southern Iowa.

The town had three bars. Alice had lived over one last year when she had lived in Downey, a sort of groovy poverty with a red shag carpet and giant concrete pillars monolithing through the main room. Too many late nights and cranked honkey tonk from below motivated her to move into a house with Melody Parker, a single teacher of special ed, when Alice was hired in Oscar Springs.

Bill's Grocery was neat and tidy, updated with wood siding that bespoke modernism. The screen door never quite shut in the summer. In the store, Alice found her roomie. Melody was petite, only coming up to Alice's shoulders. Her eyes were Goldie Hawn large, and her blond hair was Crystal Gayle long. Melody complained about conditioning. Alice complained about straightening.

"Did we run out of milk?" asked Alice.

"I was thinking pizza for supper," said Melody.

"No Tim?"

Melody flipped her hair over one shoulder. "Chores," she said. "Pizza and diet soda."

That was indeed as wild as it got for a teacher in Oscar Springs on a Friday night.

A bag of Hyland potato chips and an eight-pack of Fresca joined the Tombstone pizza in Melody's wire cart. Bernice the cashier talked over the teachers' heads as she loaded the frozen, processed dinner into a smooth paper bag. Two lanky farmers were behind them in line.

"You saw the pack over by Halcomb's?" Bernice asked.

One of the farmers nodded. "Pack leader's a mangy fellow. Big mutt, part wolf maybe."

"We think there's about twelve," said the other guy. "Tearing up cattle."

"What are you talking about?"

"Dogs," said Bernice. "Pack of wild dogs're attacking the cattle outside of town."

Alice didn't know what to say.

"Why don't you call the county?" said Melody. "Have them take care of it."

The first guy smiled, showing teeth stained by chewing tobacco. "They can't do nothing, Miss Parker. These dogs is wild."

"Best to put them out of their misery," said Bernice. "Don't want them coming into town. Already got enough strays."

A bell tinkled above the door as Alice and Melody left. "I've just about had it today," Alice said.

"Sturgeon?"

"Oh yeah. And now this. Let's shoot something!"

Melody and Alice headed down the cracked sidewalks and across the tracks. The main street had sidewalk crossings built out of thick, tarred railroad ties. Alice crinkled the bag as they walked.

"I know what you're thinking," said Melody.

"That people make their own stupid problems, and then blame the animals?"

"It's not that easy," Melody said. "The farmers don't dump the dogs, and they can't let the pack grow. They have to do something."

They passed by the American Legion building with its sagging side staircase and its homemade sign, the letters slanting downward and becoming smaller as you read from left to right. The dead gas station next to it was rimmed with dried weeds, pumps speckled with rust. Houses across from the Methodist Church showed signs of recent repair and mowed lawns.

"Wish we'd picked up some booze," said Alice. She watched Melody jiggle the key in the lock. The porch of their rental sloped slightly.

"You know teachers don't drink!" said Melody. "What are you? Some sort of pervert? Don't you remember the vows you took in college?"

Alice raised three fingers like a girl scout. "I solemnly promise to never enjoy myself again."

A meow echoed from in front of Ethel Babcock's house. Next door to the old house where Alice and Melody lived, on the corner right across from both their house and Smalleys, Ethel lived alone. They met because of Ethel's cat Tiger, a cat and a half's worth of orange tabby. Tiger had free range of the block, making his best kills in the Smalley's junky yard. Sometimes Melody and her boyfriend Tim would have to remove one of the presents that Tiger had left on the sidewalk for his owner: dead bunnies, squirrels, mice. Tiger was an excellent provider.

Melody knelt down to pet Tiger and Alice unlocked the fussy door. She took the brown bag through the living room. In the kitchen, Alice unloaded Fresca into the refrigerator. Melody cranked the dials of the oven.

Door-rattling thunder shook the front wall in the living room. Alice jumped. Melody raced across the kitchen, weaved past the couch and pulled back the beaded front door curtain.

"Oh my God," she whispered as Alice entered the room. "Abel Smalley is on our porch!"

"Open the door," said Alice.

Abel Smalley had the spare figure of someone who was engineering the destruction of his liver. His eyes were unfocused and moist, but he was angry. "I heard you want my boy to go to a shrink," said Smalley. "My boy ain't crazy. You stay away from my boy."

"Abel," said Melody, "go on home now."

"Mr. Smalley," said Alice, "I can't stay away from Junior. He'll be in my class."

"You stay away from my boy," echoed Smalley. "You tell Sturgeon to stay away from my boy. All of you, if you know what's good for you."

"Why don't you go home, Abel?" Melody called to Junior, who was half across the street. "Junior, come and take your daddy home."

Alice peered over Melody's head. Junior stood in the middle of the street, his face flushed.

"Hello, Junior," said Alice.

Junior walked slowly up the porch steps and took his dad's arm. Abel shook his hand off. "Go home, boy."

"Come on, Dad." Junior led his dad away.

Alice closed and locked the door. She hugged herself with her hands. "I'm calling the sheriff."

"Don't be stupid," said Melody. "No point blowing this up bigger than it is."

"That man is dangerous."

"That man is pathetic. He's too drunk to do anything except yell."

Alice wandered into the kitchen, wondering if something was in the water at the school that made teachers forget they were supposed to be helping kids.

— •◆• —

In the early morning, Alice stumbled through the warm glow into the kitchen. She ran her hands through the cloud of her hair to tame it, knowing it would do no good until after her shower. Not that she needed to look good for anybody on her morning run. From the refrigerator, she pulled out a carton of orange juice and moved empty Fresca bottles out of the way as she took a seat at the dining room table.

She hadn't slept well. Every noise had kept her awake. There hadn't been any fireworks over at the Smalley home, no lights, no sirens, like on a lot of nights. Alice had expected them. She swallowed back the orange juice. As she laced up her shoes, she thought about her neighbors.

Abel Smalley tinkered with cars when he was sober. He would drive his rust box down Main Street, hunched over the wheel, his eyes like tiny seed beads as he tried to navigate through the smears on the windshield and an alcoholic haze. Among the elaborate maze of old models and random parts that made up his yard he had two rusty ramps. He'd climb underneath them, sleeping in the high grass with the garter snakes, a car canopied above him.

Patrice was seldom home. She drove an Olds to and from the nightshift at the local plastics plant. Alice understood from other teachers that there had been an older sister, smart as a whip. Gone as soon as she could be gone, and a good thing. Junior spent most of his time alone with Dad.

Alice threw a sweatshirt over her head. Her running feet took her onto the cracked sidewalk. Diagonally down the road was the Smalley house, one of those gray-brown buildings rotting at the speed of rural life.

The sun was barely up. Shadows deepened the elephant's graveyard of spare parts in front of the Smalley's home like tar pits. Winches hung like nooses above spare car frames. The gravel road led past the house, across a railroad crossing as uneven as an old man's spare teeth.

The railroad split the town like a suicide scar. The business district, school, and the black tops out of town on one side. Residences on the other, a couple of churches, and that mix of prosperity and poverty, which you could only find in a town with under 600 people.

Alice's feet slapped on the gravel. Deep grass fringed the road along the ditch on the Smalley side of the street, dusty and luminous white. There were no curtains on the Smalley windows and no signs of life in the early morning. Toward the far end of the street was the school. She could see them down there, a pack of strays sprinting in the schoolyard, heading for the back, across the gravel parking lot and into the football field. She stopped and rubbed her eyes. It looked like one of the strays was a child, loping along on hands and feet, pink and nude in the early morning sun. She shielded her eyes with a hand to check what she had seen, but all the dogs had disappeared around the building into the playground area.

Clasping her hands together, she stretched her shoulders, the stretch languid like a thawing river in spring. She decided not to run toward the school. She was sure there were no feral children, but on the off chance that there were, she didn't feel like meeting one today.

Alice turned and her eyes scanned the tall grass and moved down into the ditch, and that's when her eyes met the dog's. It lifted its head and it whimpered, a whoop that cut across the morning silence, and then it breathed, rib cage barely moving.

Alice clambered down the slope, clouds of white limestone from the broad blades of grass coating her bare legs. "Hey there, boy," she soothed.

The dog tried to drag itself away with its front legs and collapsed. Underneath it, the ground was matted and slick. Alice recoiled, her fist rising to cover her mouth, nausea welling into her throat. Blood. The dog closed its eyes and panted.

Alice clambered out of the ditch and sprinted across the street back to the house. She threw the screen door open, and it spanked the doorframe. The phone book was under a stack of papers in the hall. The papers scattered like leaves as she threw them off. She ripped the pages of the phone book open. Her forefinger scanned down columns of text.

Melody raced down the stairs, clutching her robe around a t-shirt. "What the hell?"

Alice shook her head. "Not now." She ran into the kitchen and clutched the receiver of the phone out of its cradle. Cramming her fingers into the holes of the dial, it seemed an eternity as the rotary returned after each number. Alice paced while the phone rang. She twirled the cord around her fingers as she wore a path into the linoleum the length of the phone's tether.

The answering machine screeched through the nurse's recorded pleasantries and then the cheerful voice gave the vet's emergency number. She jammed her fingers again and took a deep breath as she leaned against the table, Melody watching.

The phone clicked. The answering voice was baritone. "Hello. Chris Petersen."

Alice shouted the information at him and when she had his promise he would be there in an instant, she slammed the phone back onto the wall. In the downstairs bathroom, she ripped the fluffy bath towel from the hook on the door and ran back outside.

"I'll send him over," Melody yelled after her.

Ten minutes later, she was back in the ditch. She covered the dog with the towel. She petted the dog's head. It was dying.

After an eternity, a white van pulled up beside her on the road. The vet rolled down his window. "Alice? I'm Chris."

Alice spared him a glance. He was an athletic man, the vet, tan and blond, missing his surfboard.

"Any idea what happened?"

"No." Her voice was edged with tears. "He's bleeding."

Chris opened the back of the van and came out with a muzzle and a flat carrier. He landed beside her. Speaking to the dog, he slipped the muzzle over its snout. Then he crouched down. He jimmied the carrier under the dog, which growled and yelped. He pushed the dog the rest of the way onto the carrier. "Help me carry him up," he said.

They slid the dog onto a shelf in the back of the van and Chris strapped him in. While Chris drove, Alice knelt in the back, stroking the dog's muzzle. He had black fur across his nose and left cheek, tan fur on the rest of his face, and a pink nose. For a mutt, he was adorable. Alice swallowed hard and ignored the hot tears in the corners of her eyes.

"Does he have a name?" Chris asked.

"I don't know," said Alice. "He's not my dog."

They pulled up to a square building built of concrete cinder blocks just outside of town. A Volkswagen bug waited in the parking lot and a husky mountain man climbed out. Alice wondered if the car was bigger on the inside than the outside, and if there would be other clowns emerging. "What is it?" said the man.

"Dog." Chris indicated Alice with a tilt of his head. "She found it down by Smalley's."

The large man scowled. "Why am I not surprised?" He lifted the blanket. "Chris, this is bad. We should put this one down."

"Not unless we have to," said Chris. Chris opened the glass door.

Behind the counter on the right side, an older woman, her hair piled high in a beehive, stood up. "Doc?"

"Mamie," said Chris, "you're going to see to appointments this morning while Irv and I operate. Turn the answering machine on if you're too busy."

The woman clucked, the corners of her eyes crows-feeting. "Poor puppy."

Chris and Irv angled the dog past the reception counter and through a swinging door. Alice's ears were assaulted with pathetic mews and bellowing barks.

"Do you want some coffee?" Mamie solicited.

"Yes. Can I use your phone?" While Mamie filled a Styrofoam cup, Alice called Melody.

"What kind of dog?" Melody asked.

"It's a mutt. Kind of medium-sized."

"Do you want me to come get you?"

"I'll call you."

For the next two hours, Alice sat in a plastic shell chair leafing through a tattered woman's magazine as pet carriers and dogs on leashes came back and forth. Mamie handled the cases and took the calls. When Alice exhausted the magazine, she peeled the Styrofoam cup into petals, and folded alternating ones up and down.

The big guy came out. Irv, Alice remembered. Mamie looked at him over cat eyeglasses.

"He'll make it," the big guy said. "He's a tough dog. Fifty-three stitches. No punctures to any major organs, although we had to sew lots of his insides together."

Mamie looked at Alice. "That's good news. What's his name, Miss Brubaker?"

"I don't know."

Irv sat down by her. He dwarfed the chair, overflowing onto the next one. "Stray?"

"Maybe the dog belongs to the Smalleys?"

Irv snorted. "I doubt it." He sipped coffee from a chipped mug and made a face as he forced a swallow down. "That's a good thing you did, calling Chris."

"I couldn't let it bleed to death."

"Some folks would have."

Chris came out from the back drying his hands on a paper towel. His shirtsleeves were rolled up over muscular arms. "I'm going to keep him for a while, see how he does in recovery."

"What happens to him after that?" Alice asked.

"The county'll take him," said Mamie.

"I don't like the sound of that," said Irv.

"Me neither," said Alice.

"Not this one," said Chris. "He'll come home with me. Irv,"

said Chris, "why don't you give Alice a ride home?"

"Don't trouble yourself. I'll call my roommate. I'll come back tomorrow and see about the bill."

"This one's on us," said Chris. "We take care of strays."

<hr>

As Alice tossed and turned, the sheets spiraled around her legs. The bulb of the streetlight near the house flickered on and off like a demented firefly. Somewhere around three, Alice covered her head with her pillow, but decided that she couldn't breathe like that. She battled her way out of the bed and shambled across the room to her window, opened to allow what small amount of air was circulating into her room. She wiped her forehead with a bony wrist.

The wonky streetlight strobed the Smalley house, dark and silent. Alice stealthed past the door of Melody's room and into the bathroom where she rinsed her face with cold water. Pulling the metal beads that dangled from the side of the mirror, she turned on the light, a fluorescent that made her look more like a cadaver than a living woman. "Yeah," Alice said to her reflection. "Like he'd give you a second look." She rubbed under a lower eyelid and then pulled the light off, weaving her way down the hall and back to her bed.

Alice's mother had always told her that the first year of teaching was the hardest, and Alice had had some challenges, but this second year was a real doozy. Sturgeon was a jerk, no doubt about it. It seemed like he was on a special drug for recalcitrant idiots. There were too many kids with too many problems. Mark Halcomb wasn't in her class, although he'd be missing school. In her class, there were four boys in trouble already. Joel Tate's parents were divorcing, and his mother didn't care if Joel was in school or not. Tom and Steve were thugs.

Junior was the icing on the cake. Alice wanted to help kids, but this town, the way it went through children, made her think hard about what she was doing with her life.

Her vision was hazy, so she wasn't sure at first, and her brain took a moment to crystalize the experience. Someone was looking in her window. She jumped and shouted. The figure disappeared.

"You stay away from my son! You bitch! You stay away! You tell them all! Stay away from my son! Goddamn school!" Abel Smalley yelling across the street. Then his voice was lost in howling, barking, growling. Outside the window claws crunched on the siding. A claw slash and the screen became ribbons. A dog scrabbled onto the sill, the upper part of its body half in her room, long with scruffy fur. Strobing streetlight flashed off its white teeth.

Alice screamed. She grabbed the bedside lamp and threw it at the dog. It hit the side of the wall, the pink base shattering, the extension cord crossing the room like a New Year's streamer, and the dog kept coming. Alice grabbed a book and pitched it, hitting the dog square in the face. It climbed through the window, into the bedroom. She scrabbled to the front of the bed and over the left side. The dog stood there, eyes black and red in the changing light. Then the dog launched itself at her.

Alice fell to the floor, and she kicked the dog. It flew back into the wall with a yelp, its claws raking her legs.

"Melody!" Alice yelled. "Help!"

The dog bared its teeth, scrambling on top of her. Alice jammed the remains of the lamp between its jaws. The dog bit down on the bulb and electricity sparked. Alice's vision was full of black dots and sparks burned her hands. The dog flinched and scrambled for the window, its maw smoking. Alice's hands were red as she flung the lamp away. The dog was out. Alice lurched upright. The room smelled of burning fur.

Her legs ached, and she had glass in her feet.

The dog stopped under the streetlight and howled. Alice forced her breath to slow. Out of the darkness, strays of all shapes and sizes joined the dog under the lamp, howling, growling. They all watched her window. The leader skulked forward, back toward the Smalley house.

Alice sank to the bed, her heart malleting, filling her insides with its thumping.

Melody flipped on the light switch. "What on earth?"

Alice, blinded, looked at where she thought Melody's voice had come from. She heard her voice shaking. "Dog. Outside. Lots of dogs."

"Look at you! My God! What happened to your window?"

Alice blinked, trying to clear her vision. "One was in here."

"Did it bite you?"

"It scratched me. I stepped on some glass. My hands hurt." Alice felt robotic, moving back to the window. "Are they still out there?"

"Are you crazy?" Melody grabbed Alice's hand. "Stay away from there. What if those dogs are rabid?" Melody raced to the window, closed the sash, and locked it. "We are calling the sheriff."

In fifteen minutes, they were the house in the neighborhood with the police lights flashing outside of it. An ambulance had also pulled up, and Irv stepped out of it, his heavy five o'clock shadow the only indicator that it was late.

"What are you doing here?" said Alice. "I thought you worked at the vets."

"Nope. I'm an EMT, and I specialize in people. Chris calls me in when he needs some help."

"So you're a vet too?"

"Nope. Just a specialist. Let me see those feet." Irv tweezered glass out of Alice's soles. Strong hands, yet gentle and professional. He taped an ice pack to each of her palms.

"You were lucky he didn't bite you," Irv said. "I don't think you'll be running for a bit."

Sheriff Kimball McBride leaned against the frame of the living room door and penciled his report into a notebook. "I got all the details about the dog attack. You want to add anything?"

"I heard Abel Smalley yelling," said Alice. "Then the dog came in the window."

"Don't see how that's connected." Kimball scratched his head with his pencil. "Awful sorry this happened." He wiped his high forehead with a handkerchief. Alice could see the sweat stains under the arms of his shirt. "I'd suggest keeping your window closed. You ladies thought about a dog?"

"No," said Alice. "We have not thought about a dog."

"And we are less likely to do so now," said Melody. "The stray dogs in this town are out of control. What are you going to do about this?"

"I have deputies and animal control sweeping the town. We'll find the dog. Don't worry yourself."

"It's not just about tonight." Alice grimaced and looked away as Irv pulled out another fragment of bloody glass. "The other morning, I was out running, and there was a pack down by the school." Alice almost mentioned the boy she thought she'd saw, and then decided not to. "It's dangerous."

Kimball tapped his pencil eraser, then turned to tap the tip on his notebook, over and over, tumbling the pencil with his fingers. "It is that. I would suggest you don't go out at night or early in the morning. And if you ladies don't think about a dog, maybe a shotgun with some rock salt would help."

One of the deputies came inside. "They marked their territory something awful on that side of the house."

"Another reason to keep your window closed," said Kimball.

"You ladies let us know if you see anything else suspicious. You call it in, dispatch'll contact us."

The police left. Irv put some yellow goo on the scratches on Alice's legs. "There you go. Law enforcement at its finest."

"He's going to do nothing?" Melody asked.

"Yup." Irv rolled up the tweezers he'd used in a towel and wrapped Alice's feet in gauze. "Well, first he's going to think about it and then he's going to decide he's doing everything he can already."

"Unbelievable," Alice said.

"Yeah, well, that's Oscar Springs for you. You go see about those feet and hands at the clinic first thing tomorrow. Doctor's orders."

"What about school?"

"Half a day," said Melody. "We can cover your kids for half a day."

"You know, a dog's not a bad idea," said Irv, "if it's the right kind of dog."

"I don't think so," said Alice.

"Okay, well, if you change your mind, Chris and I, we can get you set up."

As soon as Melody let Irv out, she pulled out spare bedding from the living room. "I'm thinking couch for you. Sleeping bag for me."

"I'm thinking not sleeping," said Alice. "What about that rock salt?"

Melody let a bottom sheet flutter down onto the couch cushions. "Tim will get us some. Heck, I'm thinking about asking him for a real gun. One with silver bullets."

Alice smiled. "These are dogs, not werewolves."

"Yeah, well, I'm not taking any more chances."

Alice wiped sweat off her forehead. Thelma Schwarz, second grade teacher, plopped into the chair next to her. Thelma was three years from retirement. Sweat did not dare to destroy the shellacked helmet of hair she teased into an updo every morning, grey mixed with decreasing brown. A Donna Reed dress hid her thickening body, turning it into an asset. Many of the older teachers never wore slacks and Alice wondered if this were strategic.

"Good morning, Miss Brubaker." Thelma fanned herself with a copy of the note announcing the meeting.

"What do you suppose this is about?"

Thelma glanced through the bifocal part of her glasses. "Construction," she read. "Chickenpox." She rattled the paper down to her lap. "Construction and the chickenpox."

Sturgeon, broad like a football coach, stood up from the front row of the small gathering of chairs. The school's staff, K-12, had gathered, all 26 of them. Sturgeon coughed and spoke loudly, his voice unmiked and hollow. "A couple of things have happened this week that you need to know. The first one you do know. We have chickenpox starting in the school. It's likely that it'll run rampant through the kids, but we hope we've isolated the early cases to minimize the damage." Sturgeon smiled. "Which coincidentally happen to be some of our more problematic clientele, so there is an upside. Work hard with the kids to make sure they don't get behind." Purdes snickered. Sturgeon smirked at him. "Clarification. We don't want them to get further behind."

Alice rolled her eyes, but she had to admit Sturgeon was right. Lessons went better when certain kids weren't around. There wasn't much you could do about childhood diseases. If the kids were good at picking up their make-up work, they'd be fine. With the bad kids, missing a week and a half just gave teacher a mini-vacation. Alice tuned back into the next announcement.

"...asbestos in the basement. The state has decided that asbestos is a dangerous material, and we're having it removed at Christmas break."

Thelma put up her hand. "We couldn't wait until summer?"

"I suggested it, but they weren't having any. So, here's how it's going to work. We've relocated all of Wojohowicz's art classes to the back of the home economics room temporarily. If you need supplies from downstairs, Larry and the custodians have state-issued respirator masks, so send them down."

"Halloween?" said Melody from the back of the room.

"Larry and his staff will be responsible for carrying up all your holiday decorations, so I hope you labeled them well last year." He put up large hands to calm the susurrus of sound. "The state's going to come in over Christmas, remove all the asbestos, and things should be back to normal in the New Year. That's all I got."

The teachers gathered their things. Erlene shuffled into the room, sweat dripping down her brow. She wandered to Sturgeon and handed him a note. "Wait a second," he said. He glanced the note over. "I'm sorry, but I have some bad news. Mark Halcomb passed away last night."

Alice dropped her pen and notebook. Fifteen minutes remained before the day started. "How did it happen?" she blurted out.

"He'd just gotten home," said Erlene. "There was some sort of accident. His father shot him."

"Needless to say," said Sturgeon, "counselors will be on hand for students and staff that need help, and there will be a gathering in the gym to tell the students. I'll announce that. Mr. Purdes, since Mark was in your classroom, you may want to prepare them."

Sturgeon droned on. Alice picked up her notebook and pen, and headed out to the hallways, kids drifting in. She unlocked her room, and the chatter of a new school day washed over her. Was she expected to tell the kids? This was her first student death. How would this affect how the other kids treated Junior? Alice popped into the hall and impaled the absence receipt onto the nail just above her door.

"Math," announced Alice, returning to the front of the room. There was a ruffling of papers and pages, students lifting the tops of their desks and pulling out folders, books, and worksheets. A few of the student desks were jam-packed with haphazard collections of God only knew. How could you find anything in a desk like that? "Hand up those worksheets."

"Miss Brubaker," asked Miriam Ellsworth, "why are you wearing sneakers?"

"I cut my foot running," said Alice. She gathered the worksheets and watched the kids start working at the assignment written on the board.

Alice leafed through the stack. Junior's sheet was grimy and crumpled and stuck out much like the kid himself. With the exception of his name, it was blank. "If you need help," she said, "come up to the desk and ask. Junior, you come up now."

Today Junior was wearing a t-shirt that came to his knees with some sort of brown stains on the pocket, one corner of which hung off the shirt. Alice smoothed out the crumpled paper. "Care to tell me about this?"

"I don't know," Junior mumbled. He poked a finger through a hole in the shirt, twisting the shirt around like he was wringing a bird's neck.

"What don't you know?" Alice asked. "How to add fractions?"

"I don't know."

Alice pulled a crisp extra copy from the stack in the plastic organizer on her desk. "See what you can do with this."

Junior went back to his desk. One of the boys tried to trip him, but Junior jumped over his foot. The sole of his tennis shoe flopped away, and the class laughed. Junior glowered at the boy, drew his index finger across his throat, and the other boy flipped him off.

Fifth grade, thought Alice. End of the innocence. "Joel, you will go to the office."

"But I—"

"Did I ask you to talk back to me?"

Joel stood up like a whipped dog and left.

It was always the same. The kids that were the most trouble to kids like Junior were the ones on the social ladder only a rung or two above. Town gossip pegged Joel's single mom as easy, and from the times Alice remembered her at the bar in Downey, that could be true. Another kid with another bad parent. Another kid in trouble.

"Junior," said Alice. "Take your math sheet to the resource room. I'll find you there."

When the students dismissed for recess, Alice headed to the resource room. The alphabet striped the top of the blackboard. A small carpet remnant area with some books and beanbags was occupied by a reading girl. Pat Jackson was holding up flash cards for a group studying addition. Alice searched the room but didn't see Junior.

Pat glanced up. "Junior's with Mr. Willet. Is this yours?" Pat handed Alice a paper airplane made from the math sheet.

"Can you get him to do it?"

"I can make him sit here until he's a skeleton if he doesn't," said Pat. "You know what he said? He said, 'My daddy don't want me to be in Miss Brubaker's class.'"

"Well." Alice cradled her elbow. "He's going to have to. In this thriving metropolis, there isn't another option for him."

Willet slipped out of the tiny tutoring room. Alice saw Junior over his shoulder. "Miss Brubaker? A word?" He closed the door. Willet was the counselor she had fought to get here for Junior. "We're going to pull Junior out from your classroom and in here full time. What with Mark Halcomb's death and his father—"

Alice raised a hand and spoke. "If it'll help him, I'm for it."

"I'm going to file some paperwork with the county. This is clearly a neglected child, at least. I would recommend fosterage. Right now, this room is the best place for him."

Alice headed for the office to find Joel. Finally, someone was getting Junior some help that might do him some good. Fosterage would mean getting out of Oscar Springs, and it would be good to get him away from this town, where no one particularly liked him. She knew she didn't, and that shook her assumptions about what a teacher should be. It didn't feel like victory to her, but she didn't know what would.

———◆◆◆———

The teachers' lounge smelled like the walls were built of ashtrays. Alice didn't smoke, but the omnipresent haze from the teachers that did permeated everything: the couch, the plastic tables, and if, Alice suspected, she stayed too long, Alice's insides. Alice chewed on a red pen and watched Thelma Schwartz light up. Alice worried that with the amount of hairspray Thelma used to keep her hair immobile, she might catch on fire.

Thelma offered Alice the pack, and Alice refused. Melody also shook her head.

"Now, what did you say again?" Thelma asked.

"Am I a bad teacher?" Alice tapped her pen on the table.

Thelma and Melody looked at each other, Melody rolling

her eyes like she didn't just have one more year of experience than Alice. "Well, am I? Disliking Junior, losing my temper with Sturgeon?"

"You young teachers are always so idealistic," said Thelma. "Not only are you going to dislike some students, you're also going to have favorites. You have to try to play fair, but we are human. Yelling at administrators, now that's something every teacher has to learn to do."

"I don't know," said Alice. "Maybe I shouldn't be a teacher."

"Because you can't live up to yourself? Fine. You can always marry."

"That's my plan," said Melody. "Work for a few years, then when Tim's ready, get married and get out."

"Really?" said Alice.

"Yup. Special ed is tough. Never planned to do it forever."

Thelma adjusted her glasses and peered through them. "You'll find yourself with the same problem with your children, maybe, having favorites."

Melody shrugged. "Not such a big deal. Alice, what makes you think you shouldn't teach?"

"I didn't expect things to be so difficult."

"Things?"

"The students."

Thelma tapped her cigarette on a black plastic ashtray. "Ah. The little angels. Yes."

"Don't make fun of me, Thelma."

"I'm sorry," said Thelma. "The good news is that you're a good teacher. Any teacher that doesn't ask these questions is a bad teacher or a stupid teacher."

Alice ran her fingers through her hair. "Some of them are so difficult."

Melody rested her head on her hands. "Well, you have Junior

Smalley. He's pathological."

"The other kids are blaming him for Mark Halcomb's death."

"What happened there?" Melody asked.

Thelma took a drag from her cigarette and exhaled smoke. "Erlene told me that he was out wandering in the barn, and Bill thought he was one of those wild dogs, and shot him."

"That's so sad."

"Junior didn't do it," said Alice. She waved smoke away from in front of her face. "All the kids will treat him worse, though. And it's not just Junior. There's Joel. Everyone in town knows his mother sleeps around. What kind of life does Joel have? Why don't Tom and Mary Casey's parents make their children do their homework? Why can't Nancy talk to the other girls? She's so shy, and she's afraid."

Thelma pursed her lips. "Alice, dear, listen. When you're a teacher, you know what you're getting is damaged goods, especially in a town like this one. We can't solve all the problems. That's not what teachers do. We don't have a wand, or a magic pointer, if you like. What we do is we provide what the parents don't provide, if we can. So, you give Joel and Junior the only stability they have. And you smile at Mary, so if she doesn't get that at home, she gets it somewhere in her life. What you do is make the little differences. You don't know what will affect these kids, but they have a better chance with you in their corner. That's what we do. We're in their corner." Thelma tapped a column of gray ash into the tray. "I hope I'm preaching to the choir here?"

"Yes, all right." Alice stood up and stretched. She wrinkled her face and held her wrist to her nose for the smallest of moments. Faint lavender perfume on the inside of her wrist and the ointment she was using on the burns from her palms, leftover from this morning, gave her a tiny reprieve.

"For now," said Melody. "We have this conversation like

what, every week?"

Mr. Purdes entered the room. The sound from the hall disappeared as he air-locked the lounge by closing the door. He slumped in a chair.

Thelma offered him a cigarette. He raised a barrier hand. "Mark Halcomb is the first student I've ever lost."

"Sorry," said Thelma. "That's not easy."

Thelma smoked, and Alice was hypnotized by the exhaling of smoke from her nose and mouth. Official word was that the law felt Bill Halcomb had been punished enough. Something nagged at her about the whole affair, though she couldn't quite put her finger on it.

—◆◆—

The oscillating fan sliced the air. Sweat pooled in the small of Alice's back, in the hollows of her collarbone, in between her breasts. September's last gasp was a breath of fire.

Melody wandered through the front room, gulping a glass of water. Her hair was pulled away from her face, small strands escaping and sticking to her forehead. Her hanky top flashed her belly as the fan turned her way. "You sure you don't want to come? Air conditioning!"

"No. Thanks." Alice wiped the perspiration off a bottle of Grape Crush. Melody and Tim were headed over to Richley to the movies. "Have you thought about the dog?" Two days and no more dog incidents, although a rock salt shotgun leaned against each woman's wall within arm's reach of their beds. Today the landlord had replaced the screen of Alice's window. They were still jittery every night when they went to sleep.

"Mmm," said Melody. She concentrated on her image in a mirror, the hands of a surgeon as she lined her eyes with brown pencil. "Why not? It needs a home, and we need protection."

"It's a mutt," said Alice. "Not a German Shepherd."

"It's not only the dog, is it?"

"Excuse me?"

"I think it's smart," Melody said. "If we keep the dog, you'll get to see more of that hunky vet."

"The thought had crossed my mind," said Alice.

"Good."

A horn sounded outside. Melody threw lipstick into a hand-bag and slid into platform sandals. "See you later."

"That's what I like about Tim," said Alice, her voice following Melody out the door. "He knows how to treat a lady." When the room was empty, she added, "Make sure you're back by twelve."

Alice wrangled the fan into the living room. She manhandled the La-Z-Boy toward the television. She wiped sweat from her forehead as the doorbell rang.

Alice peered out the bead curtain. Irv loomed large. She could barely see the Richley ambulance behind him.

Alice slid out the front door and onto the porch. "Hello," she said. "Nice wheels."

"Even the ambulance needs washing sometimes," said Irv. "You busy?"

"My usual date with Mary Richards," said Alice. "After that, I have a math test to check."

"Yes, then?"

"No, then."

"Chris and me, we're gonna grab some burgers at Luann's. Nothing fancy, but we wondered if you wanted to come along."

"Okay," said Alice. "Let me get my purse."

Alice slipped back in the house and changed her shirt from the sweat-soaked tank to a halter. She put a band in her hair, made sure to lock the front and the back doors, and scrambled into the ambulance on the passenger side, cranking down the window.

"So, Irv," she said as they headed down the road. "Are you from around here?"

"I grew up here," said Irv. "Went to school in Ames. Came back."

"I went to school in Ames," said Alice.

"Small world. No more trouble with the dogs." Irv said it like a statement, but Alice assumed it was a question.

"Yeah. So far. Melody and I are thinking about getting a dog, maybe if our rescue needs a home."

Irv was quiet as he parked the ambulance. In front of Luann's, Chris waited, hands shoved in jeans pockets. "Hello," said Chris. He straightened from a casual lean.

"Good evening," said Alice.

"Don't think of this as a date," said Irv. "Otherwise, we'll have to decide which one of us is paying for you."

"For a date, we'd have to go to the new Pizza Hut in Richley," said Alice. "Maybe even all the way to Des Moines." Luann's, with its plastic burger baskets and Ore-Ida fries wasn't going to impress anyone. "I'm liberated. I can pay for my own onion rings."

They settled into one of the booths. A girl that Alice recognized from the third-floor hallway gave them some menus. Irv settled on the pizza burger.

"You shouldn't eat food that's two things," said Chris. "If God had meant for the pizza burger to happen, there'd be a cut of the cow that was mozzarella."

"You eat chili dogs," said Irv.

"That's different," said Chris.

Alice sipped water from a plastic amber glass.

"Irv tells me you work at the school," said Chris.

"I teach fifth grade," said Alice.

"That's gotta be hard," said Irv. "Managing all those kids."

Alice shrugged. "It's not all that different from Chris' job. Herding cats."

Chris laughed, a kind of silent laugh where his mouth opened but nothing came out. "I hope your kids like you better than my patients like me."

"Yeah," said Irv. "They hate Chris."

"They don't understand you're trying to make them better," said Alice.

"It's not that. Chris is just special," said Irv.

"How about your patients?"

"You tell me."

A moment of silence. From the open door that adjoined onto the bar, they could hear the pings of a pinball machine.

"So, what's the story on you two?"

Chris looked at Irv. Irv raised an eyebrow back. "What'd you mean?" said Chris.

"A vet and a paramedic walk into a bar," Alice said.

"Okay," said Irv. "We were roommates in college. Chris graduated as a vet. I'm from Oscar Springs. Oscar Springs didn't have its own vet, and you can imagine that the farmers wanted one, so he moved here this fall, and I moved back here. Town this pathetic needs people to come back educated and help."

"And late at night," said Chris, "we fight crime."

"Like Batman and Robin?"

"Yes." Chris took a drink of water.

"You don't live in a bat cave?"

"Nope. I live outside of town, a big farm. Some of the strays I work on also live there, kind of an alternative to the county. I usually find homes for the pets the county usually euthanizes."

"How's our patient?" Alice asked.

Chris' jaw set. "I'm afraid he didn't make it."

A stone dropped in Alice's stomach. All that frantic work,

and the dog had died. It hit her hard. She didn't realize how much she wanted that dog to be hers until that moment. She walled away her disappointment. "His odds weren't very good," said Alice.

Irv shook his head. "Look, if you're nervous, I can lend you my dog for a while. Mary's a scrapper."

"Mary?" said Alice.

"Irv collects Marys," said Chris. "His girl and his dog are both named Mary."

"Oh."

"Mary's not my girl, Chris." Irv gulped his drink, wiped his mustache, and looked at Alice. "I don't have a girlfriend. Just to be totally clear."

Orders were taken. Alice played it safe and went for the cheeseburger and onion rings. Chris ordered the blue-plate special--roast beef, mashed potatoes, gravy, and peas and carrots. Irv had an order of fried mushrooms come out early with the drinks.

"You heard about Mark Halcomb?"

"Yup." Irv swilled back some water. "No secrets in a town this size."

Alice thought that a town this size shouldn't have this much violence. "Irv, what can you tell me about the Smalleys?"

Irv shook the mushroom basket at Chris. Chris placed a handful on a small plate. "You already know that they're low-life scum?" said Irv.

"I know that Patrice and Abel have drinking problems."

"Same thing," said Irv.

"Alice," said Chris, "I don't know how to ask you this. What do you think happened to that dog?"

Irv took a long drink of water. "Chris, you think Junior cut the dog up, don't you?" said Irv.

"Yeah," said Chris.

"Shit," said Irv.

"That poor kid," said Alice.

"Poor kid?" repeated Irv.

"Yeah, poor kid," said Chris. "His dad is the biggest asshole in seven counties."

"That poor kid is old enough to know right from wrong." Irv pressed the batter crumbs into his fingers and licked them off.

"He's got a home environment that teaches him wrong is right," said Alice.

Chris took a meditative drink of Coke. "There's a social worker in Richley," said Chris.

Alice emptied a bottle of soda into a glass of ice. The fizz sounded in the silence and pop fountained into the air. "The school's getting him help through the local education agency. Principal Sturgeon wants us to keep him at school as much as we can."

"Chris," said Irv, "we should talk to Junior and Abel about the dog."

"I've had better luck talking to Patrice," said Alice. "Abel gets riled up."

Chris peered over the glass at her. "Abel's been bothering you?"

"Just the once." Alice shifted in her seat. "Just told me to leave Junior alone."

"There's more to it than that," said Irv. "Abel and I go back. In an I-hate-your-guts kind of way. You let us know if he gives you any more trouble."

"Thanks," said Alice.

"Alice has been having trouble with the strays." Irv finished his water in another gulp.

"Yeah, I heard about that," said Chris. "No more after that first night? I'm pretty sure you haven't had any more trouble." He and

Irv nodded at each other, like they shared some macho secret.

"No more attacks," said Alice. "We're still having some territory marking."

"That can happen," said Chris. "Your house is now a beacon for everyone's dog."

"Like a fire hydrant," said Irv. "Like I said, we're talking to Abel. Maybe you'd like to borrow Mary?"

"Mary's a good idea," said Chris. "She's a sharp dog."

—◆◆—

Students shuffled into their seats after recess, stowing jackets in the side lockers of the classroom. Joel was out with the chickenpox. He was the only one gone today. Apparently, Sturgeon's strategy was working so far. Junior shuffled in with the rest. Alice cocked her head his direction, but he ignored her. She started stacking worksheets on her desk and opened her mouth to get the class' attention.

Thump! Alice looked up. Junior lay face down between the third and the fourth rows of desks. A cluster of boys were trying not to giggle. Alice barked at them. "Who did that?"

Junior stood up. His eyes lined to slits as they went from one boy to the next. Steve turned red trying not to laugh.

"Steve," said Alice. "Mike. Tom. You three. Office right now."

Tom's mouth gaped open. "I didn't do anything."

"Save it for Mr. Sturgeon," said Alice. "Va-moose. All of you."

The boys shuffled out. Removing those three took the stinger out of the wound, but the wound still remained.

"Junior," said Alice. "Why are you here?"

"Mr. Sturgeon said I had to be here."

As they worked their way through fractions, Junior leaned his pudgy cheek into his palm. When Alice asked him a question, silence followed. The three horse boys of the Apocalypse returned with a note from the principal's office, smirking. Alice's gaze lasered sniggering boys into sobriety. Later, they would scrape dead gum off the desks after school. While the students answered their worksheets, Junior put his head down and closed his eyes. Alice called Junior to her desk.

Junior didn't move. "My dad says I'm not supposed to talk to you." His voice was flat, matter of fact.

"Right. Your turn. Office." Alice returned her attention to the spelling list, writing the words on the board, her chalk skittering and crumbling as she pressed too hard. The bell rang. Time to send the kids to art and have it out with Sturgeon about Junior. As soon as they were gone, Alice set her jaw and walked opposite lines of students, through the hall littered with construction paper leaves, and into the office.

Erlene smiled. "Hey, honey." She shifted her bulk from the desk to the typewriter and began to thread a form into it.

"Is Junior with Sturgeon?"

"Junior didn't show up here."

Alice blew air out of puffed cheeks.

"Do we have an AWOL?" Erlene asked.

Alice rapped on the principal's door.

"I wouldn't bother him." Erlene's chest puffed out as she maneuvered to intercept, but Alice was faster.

Inside, Sturgeon was bent over some paperwork. "Miss Brubaker. Do you mind?"

"Mr. Sturgeon." Alice closed the door, shutting Erlene out. She stopped grinding her teeth. "Did you have a conversation with Mr. Willet yesterday? About Junior Smalley?"

"Yes."

"And?"

"I talked Willet out of it."

Alice leaned toward Sturgeon. "Talked him out of what, exactly?"

"We don't need any student of ours being dragged into the state system."

Alice stood up and ran fingers through her unruly hair. "Junior is a kid who needs some serious help."

"Perhaps if you applied yourself harder to the problem, we could manage it." Sturgeon tapped his pen on the stack of papers on his blotter.

Alice took a breath. Control. It was all about control. "My job is to teach twenty children, Mr. Sturgeon. At the very least, Junior needs special education. He's behind everyone else. And he is violent."

"Calm down, Ms. Brubaker," said Sturgeon. "Hysteria has never served our purposes."

Hysteria? Alice rubbed her chin. "Walt, I think Junior's mutilating animals. I think he cut up a dog."

"Yes. I've heard from Miss Parker you've been having trouble with some of the stray dogs."

"This dog wasn't one of the pack. Ask Doc Petersen. He'll tell you all about it."

Sturgeon leaned back in his chair. "What you don't understand, Alice, is that this isn't Des Moines. People in this town, we try to get along. We try not to make waves."

Alice hit the desk and was reminded of how hard the desk was. "How can you not do something?"

Sturgeon steepled his fingers and narrowed his eyes. "The matter is closed. Junior will stay in your class. He will consult with Mr. Willet, but we aren't pulling him out of school. The previous arrangement stands. I believe we've compromised enough."

Alice opened her mouth.

Sturgeon stared at her and carefully pronounced each word of what he said next. "I would hate to have to let you go. I would suggest you leave this alone."

Alice closed her mouth. She felt her cheeks flush. She walked out of Sturgeon's office and picked up Erlene's phone. "Do you have the Smalley's number?"

"Don't do anything rash, honey."

"I've got to find where he is, don't I?" said Alice through clenched teeth.

The phone picked up after the sixth ring. "Hello?" Patrice sounded like she'd been unconscious.

"Mrs. Smalley? This is Alice Brubaker, Junior's teacher. Has Junior come home?"

There was movement. A click and some sound smudges. Some confused voices in the background. And then, after some more sound smudges, Patrice picked up the phone. "No," she said. "He ain't here. Can't you teachers keep track of him?"

"This is serious, Mrs. Smalley. He's missing."

There was a mental shrug. At least, that's what Alice imagined. "We're gonna be moving on soon, Miss Brubaker. No reason for you to worry about Junior anymore."

"For God's sake!" Alice's temper snapped like a cheap pencil. "Someone has to. Neither you nor his father seem to!"

The door to Sturgeon's office opened. Erlene's chest heaved up and down like the prow of a ship on a swelling ocean. Alice was about to slam the phone down when she heard the tiniest of voices come out of the receiver.

"Can I come to see you at the school, Miss Brubaker?"

Alice jammed the phone back to her ear. "What?"

Patrice's voice was a whisper. "Tomorrow. I gotta work tonight. Tomorrow."

Adrenaline bled out of Alice, leaving her deflated like a balloon. "Yeah. I mean yes, Mrs. Smalley. I'll expect you tomorrow afternoon. Goodbye." She replaced the phone in the cradle.

Sturgeon stretched. "You never know what's going to work with parents, do you?" He disappeared back into his office.

———•••———

Tim met Alice at the end of the block before she reached the yard. He was a compact farmer, his feed cap pulled low, dirty with the dust of a day at harvest. "You wanna go in the backdoor today."

"What's up?" Alice tried to see over his shoulders.

"Tiger is all over your yard." Tim shoved his hands in his pocket and studied the pockmarks in the concrete sidewalk.

"All over?" Alice's voice stopped as she fitted together what Tim had said.

Tim rubbed his hand over the stubble of his chin. "Probably the dogs that attacked the house. I'm cleaning him up."

"Poor Ethel!"

"Melody's over there. You can go over if you want."

Alice stared at the Smalley home. Anger flared into her throat. Damn it. Was it Junior who'd cut the cat up? Or was Tim right, that it was the dogs? "No," said Alice. "Not right now." Alice circled the house, avoiding the front, concentrating on the slope that led to the backdoor. She fought with the key, with the stiff door and squeezed through storage boxes into the kitchen. Alice threw her purse over the back of the chair. Then she punched the kitchen wall. She shook her hand. "Ow! Jesus! Shit!"

Alice breathed. Okay. It had been quite a year so far. She'd call her mother and they'd talk about anger management.

The phone rang. She snatched it up with her uninjured hand. "Yeah?"

"Alice? Irv. You okay over there today?"

"Hey, Irv. No, I'm not okay. I was thinking about Mary, about your offer."

"Something else happen?" Through the phone, she could hear the pause, the worry.

"Someone's killed Tiger, our neighbor's cat. Tim thinks those wild dogs. I think Junior. Is Mary a big dog?"

"Big enough. Wiry. I'm on double shift," said Irv. "I can bring her around if you want to meet her. Thursday?"

"Deal."

"You gonna be okay?"

"Yeah." Alice wasn't certain about that. "Yeah. I'll see you then."

❖

Patrice Smalley didn't show up for her conference on Wednesday, and Alice went home half an hour late. Alice could raise no one calling the Smalley home. She wondered if they had gone. Melody had left her a note taped to the front door. Chris had called and asked for Alice to stop by the vet's office. She drove out, her mind flipping through where to go next with the Smalleys. Maybe she should just pop next door for a cup of sugar. Yeah. That'd be perfect. She went into Chris' air conditioned office.

"Dr. Petersen is with a customer," said Mamie. "You can have a seat."

Alice drummed her nails on the counter. "He called me," said Alice. "Would you let him know I'm here?"

"Certainly, Miss Brubaker." Mamie rattled her arrival into the phone and then turned toward a metal cabinet and pulled a file with vigor.

Alice leafed through the same shabby *Women's Day* she had when they bought the dog in for his surgery. Mamie helped an elderly lady with a pixie bob and a cat carrier negotiate the door. The cat inside yowled like Satan had given it a feline leukemia shot. Mamie plastered the angelic smile of customer service onto her lips. "Doc says you can go on back."

Alice passed through the swinging door. To the right, there was an examination room with a silver table bolted to the floor. On the counter along the wall was a scale, a variety of pill bottles, and syringes. As she rounded the corner, she entered a kennel. Dogs rested in a variety of wire cages. Some had apparent signs of medical care, like casts, or cones about their heads. Others barked and yowled impediment free. Slightly behind that room was what looked like a walk-in closet. Alice caught a glimpse of empty containers. The storeroom smelled like animal kibble and alcohol.

Chris was chatting with a golden retriever, who looked like he'd been sewn together out of other dogs. While the stitches were mostly removed, he had pink scars rivering among his short fur, one around the top of his right forepaw, and another that curved up either side of his belly. A scar striped his nose. "You'll be running around in no time," said Chris, patting the dog's head.

"Wow," said Alice. "What happened to him?"

"Hit by a car. Melville likes chasing cars and this time it caught up with him."

The dog, tail between his legs, stepped toward Alice, and then stopped.

Alice crouched down and waited. "What can I do for you?" she asked, her voice gentle.

The dog put his muzzle under her hand and Alice stroked it, the short hairs tickling her fingertips. Something was missing. "No cats?"

"We don't keep cats and dogs together. There's another room for them."

"So, what did you want to see me about?"

"I'm heading out to Halcomb's. I know they'd like a chance to thank you, you know, about Mark."

"I don't know about that. Not with the way things turned out."

"No, they understand. You're the teacher who got him to the doctor when Junior bit him. Bill asked me especially." Chris glanced at his watch. "On my way to check out some calves."

Alice mulled it over. "I've never seen a cow diagnosed."

Chris rubbed his chin. "Your lucky day," he said.

Alice watched him walk out of the room, her eyes roaming. Melville winked at her, at least she thought he did. She shook her head. "You understand what I'm saying?"

Melville shook his head. Alice headed outside, where Chris was loading up his van. "Chris, Melville just winked at me."

"Dogs can wink. It means he feels playful. You ready?"

Alice climbed into the front of the van. Chris firmed up the afternoon schedule with Mamie, and then joined Alice. "Today's a nice change," said Chris. "These days when I go on a large animal call, it's usually damage."

"Wild dogs?"

"Yup." Chris paused at a stop sign and then rolled onto gravel.

"I wish we had a good solution for that. It's inhumane to shoot them."

"You still feel that way, even after one tried to rip into your house?"

"I'm saying it's not their fault."

"We have to do something. The cows suffer if something isn't done. I'm trying to get the town council to buy some tranquilizer guns."

"You don't want them to shoot the wild dogs either," said Alice.

"I don't want the farmers to shoot them," said Chris. "There are better ways to handle them."

Chris pulled into a driveway and drove the van around to a red barn. Alice reminded herself of what the Halcombs had been through, were going through, and hoped that her visit wouldn't renew their pain.

Out of the back of the truck, Chris pulled several large baby bottles and a jug of water. "Do you know what scours are?"

Alice shook her head.

"Sort of like cow flu," said Chris. "Two of the little calves here have it. When Mom's teats get dirty, calves pick up the bacteria. It's hard for ranchers to notice everything when the herd's out in the field. Luckily, Halcomb keeps a pretty good eye on his cattle. He caught these cases early."

They went into the barn and were hit with a pleasant smell of grassy hay and earthy cow. Stalls were scarred on the sides but lined with clean straw. A thin man pulled one square palm out and shook Chris' hand. He was watching Alice as he did it.

"Bill," said Chris, "this is Alice Brubaker."

Halcomb's voice was husky, like he was getting over a cold. "Miss Brubaker, I want to thank you for what you done for my boy."

"I'm sorry about what happened."

The emotions reflected in Halcomb's eyes dimmed, like he pulled a blind to keep the light in. "Thank you." He turned to Chris. "The calves are in those stalls."

"Right." The two men stood, studying straw on the floor, Halcomb's thumbs in his back pockets.

"Don't do anything rash," said Chris.

"I won't. I thought about everything." Halcomb adjusted his feed cap and headed out to see to his cattle.

Chris entered one of the stalls. A small calf wobbled on spindly legs. Her large brown eyes were moist. Chris pinched the cow's eyelid and the little calf bawled. "Good," said Chris.

"Not too serious yet."

"He means about the Smalleys, doesn't he?" Alice crossed her arms. "Chris, what's he going to do?"

"I don't know. If the school would do what you wanted, that might be enough for Bill. He sees Junior needs help even though he blames him."

"Is he right to blame Junior?"

Chris shook one of the bottles. "I can tell you this. Mark would never have been in danger if Junior hadn't bit him."

"Because?"

"Alice," said Chris, "ever bottle fed a calf?"

"Don't try to change the subject."

"Subject changed. You want to feed this little girl here?"

"I don't know. I'm a city girl."

"Des Moines? Big metropolis." Chris handed her a bottle of the clear liquid. "You're up to it. I'm checking out calf number two in the next stall."

The calf's jaws wrapped around the nipple of the bottle. The force of its sucking almost pulled the bottle out of Alice's hands. It slurped. Alice looked into its smooth brown eyes, its long lashes. "Say there," she said, "no need to be greedy. Plenty to go around."

Halcomb came back in and followed Chris into the next stall. They talked about how much of the electrolyte solution to give to the calves and about a pregnant heifer that Chris promised to look at before he left. Yes, there had been wild dog sightings out here, and Halcomb had taken a few shots at them. They were younger now, hungrier. Not like the old days when they were pests, not predators.

The calf finished, and Alice petted the soft hide, smooth like a suede jacket. The calf bawled again. She shushed it. It stumbled on spindly legs and lay down.

"You about done there?" Chris shouted over the stall.

"Yes. All I have here is sleepy cow."

"Alice? Would you go to dinner with me?"

Alice peered over the stall. "Depends," she said, keeping her voice even. "You promise to take me to the Pizza Hut in Richley?"

"Only the best."

Sturgeon mentioned in a teacher's lounge bulletin that, regardless of Mark Halcomb's funeral, he would appreciate it if the students' routines would return to normal as soon as possible. In spite of his wishes, the atmosphere in the school remained edgy. Even though Bill Halcomb had killed his own son, the kids had it in their heads that if Junior hadn't bitten Mark, he'd still be alive, and worse still, they concocted all the ways Junior could take the blame. Rumors in the halls and on the playground were that Junior was going to be taken to juvenile detention or jailed for murder or killed by Bill Halcomb.

Thursday school was a half-day because of the funeral, school starting in the afternoon. Alice took the students who had signed permission slips from their parents. The boys that had bullied Junior were missing, all down with the chickenpox.

Alice was proud of her students. They were respectful and stoic. Organ music wheezed over them. Alice watched Bill's wife, Sally, tears running down her tanned face, her mascara streaking, her nose red. Losing a child had to be the worst thing, her mother had said. Since she had started working with kids, she agreed.

"Miss Brubaker?"

Alice looked at Hodges, the soft undertaker, a plump pillow of a man in a sober suit. His hair was slicked back, and he fidgeted with his hands, pulling on stubby fingers. "I was wondering if the students would like to view the casket."

She glanced back over the kids. That was a parental decision, not an educational one. "No, Mr. Hodges, I don't think so. But could I?"

Mr. Hodges offered his arm, and Alice rested her hand in the crook of it. He left her at the aisle. She felt all the eyes of Oscar Springs following her to the coffin, which she kept her own eyes on, so no one would notice she noticed that they were watching her with intense scrutiny. She stood over Mark Halcomb, smaller here than when he was alive, cinched up to the neck in a blue suit, black shoes, a dark tie, the cherry birthmark even brighter, in spite of the fact that the funeral home had tried to cover up the deformity on his face with makeup, making it look more like the gradation of fur on the rescued dog's face.

Which was exactly the same pattern. In the same place.

The music faded away, and Alice stood there with the coffin. She grabbed the boy's hand, cold, and slid the sleeve back. There were scars on Mark's arm, and stitch marks. She stepped away from the coffin and the organ music rushed back in. The next people were standing behind her, waiting their turn, their faces angry with her for holding them up.

"Excuse me," said Alice. She walked back to her students.

They couldn't be the same. But they were the same. Mark Halcomb. The same scars. The same face? Alice fanned herself with the program book. She'd seen a boy running with the dogs. Not Mark, but a boy running with the dogs.

Two rows down, Sturgeon turned, adjusting his tie and staring right at her with narrowed eyes.

Outside of the church, she cornered Sheriff McBride. "I need to talk to you," she said. She had turned her students over to Mrs. Yost, who walked them down the street, like a line of ducklings, back to the school. "Kimball, I need to talk to you right now about Mark Halcomb."

Kimball didn't look at her, searching for something over her shoulder. "What can I do for you, Miss Brubaker?"

"Did you ever get those dogs?"

"Sure," said Kimball. "We seem to have a neverending supply, though."

"Did you ever notice anything funny about our dogs?" What was Kimball looking at? Alice turned. Sturgeon sauntered up, the casual walk of the jock turned administrator. She wondered how much menacing he'd done in his career with that walk.

"You answer me, Kimball McBride. Those dogs," she whispered. "They aren't dogs, are they?"

Kimball cleared his throat.

"Alice," said Sturgeon, his voice gentle. "You seemed very affected in there. Can I walk you back to the school?"

"Is there a problem here, Kimball?"

Irv was there, and Alice let out the breath she didn't know she was holding.

Kimball studied Irv and then studied Sturgeon. Alice hadn't noticed before how tall Sturgeon was. Irv was the wider of the two, but Sturgeon could look Irv in the eye without much effort. "Miss Brubaker is upset," said Kimball.

"Yeah, well, it's a funeral, isn't it? You okay, Alice?"

"I'll be fine."

Irv nodded, once. "Sturgeon."

"I don't think we've met?"

"Nope," said Irv. "We haven't." The two men stared at each other.

Melody ran down the church steps. "Come on," she said to Alice. "We've got kids waiting." Melody grabbed Alice by the arm and tugged. Alice glanced over her shoulder. Sturgeon was the first one to look away in the staring contest.

"What was that all about?" Melody flipped her hair over her shoulders. The wind blew it forward, like a veil between her and Alice.

"I…" Alice stopped. She swallowed. She had to tell someone. "That dog Chris and I saved? Did you notice the fur pattern on its face?"

"I didn't see the dog." Melody used her scarf to tie up her hair.

"That dog and Mark Halcomb have the same birthmark. Mark is covered in scars and stitches."

Melody bit her lower lip. "You think Mark and the dog are the same? Wow. That's an odd thought, right?"

"Okay," said Alice. "It is odd. But why does this town have so many strays?"

"Look, Alice, you're upset. It didn't help that Irv and Sturgeon postured all over each other back there."

"I think something's going on."

Melody touched Alice's arm tentatively. "Honey…"

"I know what I saw."

"Yeah." Melody led them off the sidewalk and into the street, so they could avoid the hill with the broken sidewalk, and take it easy on Alice's feet, in heels for the first time since the dog attack. "Listen, Alice. This is only going to make you look nuts."

Alice did a double take. "Excuse me?"

"Your crusade about Junior Smalley, well that's important. But this, this is another thing. Mark and the dog aren't the same. They can't be. What you think you saw, well, I will grant you that the dog attack was horrible. Tiger too. Don't you think maybe you're kind of stressed?"

"You've noticed things too. I know you have."

"Yes, I have. I'm just saying step back and breathe. Cool it." Melody pushed her hair behind her ears. "At least the Smalleys are gone."

———•••———

Four dogs, two older and two younger, scampered across the gravel road in front of the school through the autumn leaves in the yard across from it. Alice and Melody glanced at each other and stepped back into the building. One of the dogs, brindled with a bulldog nose, peed against the door of the building and sniffed along at its base.

Two girls tried to get out, but Melody blocked their way. "Wait," said Melody.

Alice glanced out the window. The dog took off running, back toward the practice field where the rest of the pack had gone. It became the janitor's problem. Melody let the girls out, and she and Alice followed.

"The glamorous life in Oscar Springs," said Melody.

"That's because no one in this town wants to take responsibility for anything."

Melody headed up the cracked sidewalk on the left side of the street, the one that tried to conform to a hill, but failed. "Still upset?"

"Don't tell me you can sleep at night." Alice glanced over her shoulder, back at the school. No sign of the dogs.

"I won't," said Melody.

Alice nodded. "What happened to Junior Smalley? We tried to get him the help he needs, but no! Sturgeon wants to keep it quiet. Now Mark Halcomb is dead, and where is Junior?"

"Not our problem anymore," said Melody. "They're gone. He hasn't been in school. No lights at the house. Gone."

"Why don't you care?"

"I care! Junior's got to be in another school with a better principal. This could be the best thing for everyone."

Alice blinked. There might be something to that.

Two boys were picking on a smaller boy across the street. "Hold on," said Melody. Melody ran ahead down the hill, yelling at them.

Alice leaned on one foot, waiting under the big tree at the top of the hill. Her feet hurt. She shouldn't have worn her stupid heels to the funeral that morning if they were going to walk on the cracked sidewalk, which they did every stupid day anyway. Everything was wrong. She was angry at everyone. The school administrators were like freaks from that novel about the perfect robot wives who wanted to pretend problems didn't exist. Alice took a deep breath.

Melody came back. "They won't do that again in a hurry." They started home again. "I have some beer at the house. Would that help?"

"Yes. By the way, Irv's coming over tonight. Bringing Mary, his dog. If we like her, she'll stay with us."

"The strays won't rip her up?"

"Irv thinks not."

"Alice, you are not spoiling for choice. The man mountain or the hunky vet. How're you gonna choose?"

When they turned the corner, they were downtown. Green leaves, some turned around the edges, fell off the trees, swirling in the middle of the sidewalks and road. In front of their house was the Richley ambulance. Melody's pace quickened. "You don't think something happened to Ethel?"

Alice shook her head and hiked the strap of her handbag up on her shoulder. "That's the man mountain's wheels."

Irv leaned against the side of the ambulance. Beside him was a brown whippet, all angles and sharp bits. The dog lowered the flaps of her ears and glanced up at Irv with warm brown eyes.

"Ladies," said Irv. He had five o'clock shadow and circles

under his eyes.

"Hey, Irv," Melody snapped her fingers and popped her other hand over the top, spreading her arms after the gesture. "Did you punch Sturgeon?"

"What is with that guy?"

"Too much testosterone," said Melody.

"Yeah, well, if he gives you any more trouble."

"Just start going to school with Alice. I'm sure she could use a bodyguard."

Alice's cheeks pinked. "Let's leave that topic behind."

Irv nodded. "I hear you and Chris are going out this weekend."

"That's right," said Alice.

"My condolences," said Melody to Irv.

Irv shook his head. "The battle might be over, but not the war. You ladies should meet Mary." Irv whistled through his teeth.

Mary barked and extended a paw to Alice. Alice fell into the big brown eyes. She rubbed Mary's head. "Are you a good girl?"

Mary barked.

Irv pursed his lips. "Careful, Alice, Mary doesn't like to be talked down to. Just talk to her like you'd talk to me, and you'll get along fine."

"Mary, thank you for staying."

Mary acknowledged Alice with a bark and ran off to the back of the house.

"Let me guess," said Alice. "She's checking the perimeter."

"That's right."

"I'll be in the kitchen, if either of you want a beer," said Melody. "Come along whenever."

Alice watched her go. "That was the strategic withdrawal, in case you missed it."

"Sure," Irv said. "Don't let Mary fool you. She's a tough dog in spite of what she looks like. Fast. Dangerous."

"Dangerous?"

"To bad dogs."

"And she's just a dog?"

Irv started. "What do you mean by that?"

"Irv, something really, really weird is going on here. Mark Halcomb—"

"Listen." Irv scratched the back of his head. "Now that the Smalleys are gone, it's gonna be okay."

"So Melody says. What do you mean by that?"

"This dog problem, it's gonna be over really soon. You'll see."

"What are you not telling me?"

Irv turned to her. "Listen, Alice, all you need to know is that things are going to be normal really soon."

"So, you know that Mark Halcomb was that dog?"

"Where'd you get that idea?"

"And that Junior had something to do with him turning into a dog?"

"Woah. Stop. I didn't say anything like that at all."

"You don't have to. You're from this town, aren't you? So, why the Hell would you want to talk about this? This is some weird secret you have, right? The Smalleys turn people into dogs, and everybody covers up for them?" The ridiculousness of what she had just said hit her like a sledgehammer. "Except you all hate the Smalleys. And people don't turn into dogs."

"Alice, let me try to explain. A small town is like a family. You hate it when weird Uncle Benny comes over for Thanksgiving, but you don't tell him that."

"That's bullshit, Irv. You all come down on the Smalleys, all the time."

"Yeah, okay, but you can do that in the family. However, you get defensive when someone from outside the family says something about Uncle Benny, even if you know it's true. He is your uncle."

"Fine." Alice leaned against the ambulance, crossing her arms. "If Uncle Benny needs help with his weirdness problem, you let it ride?"

"He *is* your uncle.

"We had a word for that in psychology class. We called that enabling.

"I took psychology, okay? I don't agree with it, Alice. I'm just telling you how I think it works."

"You're in on it?"

"No. I'm on Mary's side. You've got to trust me when I tell you it's over."

"Mary's side?"

Irv winced.

"She's not a dog?"

"Define dog."

"Irv—"

Irv was frowning, looking like Alice felt. "So, you've made a choice?"

"I don't follow," said Alice.

"Chris, I mean. You're going out with Chris."

"I'm going for pizza with Chris. That doesn't mean we're an item."

"Uh-huh."

"Look, you didn't answer my question about Mary. I don't think I'm obliged to give you any details about Chris."

"Fine."

"Fine."

Mary ran up the side of the yard and stopped on a dime at the edge of the road. She watched the Smalley house, her ears flattened.

Irv fidgeted. "You're going to take this the wrong way, but

maybe you don't want to get involved with Chris."

"Because?"

"It's not a good idea. He's not from around here."

"Neither am I. I'm beginning to see that as a strength."

"I mean in a different way than you."

"Maybe that's okay. Maybe he's not some small-town weirdo who's telling me to ignore what I'm seeing."

Mary ran back to Irv, who rubbed her head. She raced into the house through the open front door. "Look, Alice, just think twice about Chris. That's all. I want you to be safe."

"But not safe so that you'd tell me anything, right?"

"I won't be around to protect you if something happens."

"What?" Alice poked Irv in the chest. "Listen, maybe I want something to happen. How bad can Chris be if you're hanging around him all the time?"

"That's different," said Irv.

"What's wrong with Chris?"

Irv looked away. "Tell Melody I had to get going. You and Mary, you'll get along fine."

Alice watched Irv climb back into the ambulance and drive off.

———◆•◆———

Mary preferred Melody to Alice straight off. When they were checking papers at the kitchen table, Mary settled closer to her, watching Alice with what Alice was sure was anger.

Melody stretched. "I before e except after c, you little genius-es. That's all I ever asked. Can you deliver? No." She stood up. "That's all I can take."

Alice pushed back from her own math worksheets. "You notice we get a dog, and she likes you?"

Melody shrugged. She patted Mary's head and the pert ears

straightened more. "It's obvious. She's jealous of you."

"Uh-huh. Why?"

"Pets get like that. Irv likes you. There you go."

Mary is the name of Irv's girlfriend and Irv's dog. Hadn't Chris said something like that?

Melody walked into the living room. "Look," said Alice, staring at Mary. "I don't know exactly what's what anymore, but I'm not interested in Irv, okay? Too many secrets in this town for me to be interested in anyone from here."

Mary sighed, a doggy snort, rose languidly and trotted after Melody.

———◆•◆———

Date night with Chris was welcome when it came. Now, as Alice finished her eyeliner, Mary glanced up from lying on Alice's bed. "What do you think?" askeds Alice.

Mary put her head back down with a doggie sigh.

"I hope his reaction is better than yours," Alice said. She patted her hair one more time, spritzed some holding spray on, and headed out to the living room. "You know I suspect you're a person, don't you?"

Mary ignored her.

"Girl," said Melody from her vantage point on the couch, "you look good!" She snuggled into the crook of Tim's arm.

Tim gave Alice a thumbs up.

Alice twirled for them. She liked the orange dress. It was a polyester number with a clingy skirt, making the most out of her slim hips and modest bust. Better than the dress, though, was that she had managed to straighten her hair into submission. It had been whipped into a low chignon. Melody's suggestion of ironing it flat, even though it had taken two hours, had worked. She held a sequined white clutch. "Too much for

Pizza Hut?"

"You can never overdress for a first date."

Through the window, Alice saw Chris coming up the walk. She slung her trench coat over an arm and met him on the porch.

Alice let Chris help her down the wooden steps. Tonight, she didn't mind. Her sandals were a little higher than the shoes she was used to wearing these days, strappy and disco.

"You look nice," Chris said.

"You too," Alice returned. He did, wearing dress pants and a silk shirt. His hair was parted in the middle and feathered back, and he smelled like Old Spice.

He opened the car door for her. She slid in and he circled around to the other side. "I wondered if we'd be taking the van," Alice asked.

"Or the ambulance?" Chris shifted the car into gear. "The Dodge Charger. For guys that are compensating. It's Irv's."

Alice frowned. "You're hard on him."

"He can take it. Besides, I hear that you were pretty hard on him when he brought Mary over."

"We'll get to that." Alice fiddled with the radio, stopping when she heard Neil Diamond croon. "Is this okay?"

"Sure."

"So," said Alice. She let the purse slide down the side of the bucket seat. "Mark Halcomb's funeral. Didn't see you there."

"Meant to be. Horse emergency at Radcliff Ranch. Animals have lousy timing."

"Junior's disappeared. Patrice stood me up for a conference. I hear that they've moved on."

"If that's true," said Chris, "Oscar Springs will be happy to see them go."

Alice licked lipstick off her teeth, hoping that Chris hadn't seen it. "I'm ashamed to admit it. My class runs better without Junior there. You always have to sit on him. You know it's not his fault entirely, but sometimes it doesn't feel you can do much for rotten students but put them out of their misery." She glanced at the shoulder of the road as it rocketed by.

Chris nodded. "Kind of like those wild dogs."

Alice noted the same grim crease between his eyebrows. "Mark Halcomb and that dog?"

"Yes?"

"You know they're the same?"

"Yes."

Alice blinked. "Okay, then. Good. It's nice of you not to be evasive, or to treat me like I'm the one with the problem. That's a welcome change. I know it's a farfetched idea, but I've been seeing some odd things, and then at the funeral I noticed the scars. Mark's birthmark and the dog's fur patterns were the same. So, what really happened?"

"After the operation, I took Mark to my house to heal up. You know I keep some of my special cases there. Mark ran for home. Bill shoots wild dogs who try to mess up his cattle. He shot Mark, and Mark reverted to normal."

"Chris," Alice said. "Why was Mark Halcomb able to turn into a dog? Was it Junior?"

"Now," said Chris, "that's the part I'm not sure of. Irv thinks it was Junior."

"Junior bit him?"

"Could've been. I think more likely Abel."

"Abel's a dog?"

"Maybe you'd call him a part time dog? When I first set up practice, Abel made a lot of the wild dog pack out of his buddies. The town puts up with them, but the farmers don't."

Alice shuddered. "And the police?"

"Killing a wild dog is killing a man. Cops don't do that. And as long as they don't see it's a person, they let the farmers do what they want."

"So, it's like being a werewolf or something?" Alice turned off the radio. "Why don't the police arrest the farmers if they know?"

Chris looked ahead, his mouth a grim line. "A cover up. The cops never see a human body. It's easy to look the other way when you don't see a body and people you don't care for disappear."

"Jesus," said Alice. "This is one messed up town."

"Oh yeah," said Chris. "What I don't get is why Mark didn't heal up." Chris shifted the car. "Like creatures like that do in movies. Mark was cut up and didn't heal."

"Like Tiger. Although Tiger wouldn't heal up."

"Tiger?"

Alice explained. Chris frowned. Alice turned off the radio. "How do you know so much about um…weredogs, Chris? Do they train you for that at the vet school?"

Chris had an edge to his laughter. "Kind of. Yeah."

"Okay, so," Alice floundered for some words. "Why don't they arrest Abel? Keep him from making the dogs?"

"Can't exactly hold a trial for Abel because he makes people into wild dogs. I don't think Mark was Abel. Mark isn't Abel's style. Never heard of Abel abusing any kids but his own."

Alice was all too familiar with that. She nodded curtly. "And if the family is gone, it's not the town's problem anymore, is that it? Is that why they left?"

Chris shrugged. "Maybe. Bill Halcomb's problem, though. You might think Bill Halcomb got what he deserved. Shooting dogs and one just happens to be his boy. I know he has regrets, but up to now, he's been as bad as the rest of them."

"So what do we do now?" Alice asked.

"You keep teaching kids and doing what you do. Me, I try to

figure out who turned Mark Halcomb into a dog."

"I think it was Junior," Alice said. "He bit Mark Halcomb."

Chris nodded. "I'll look into that. If anyone'll know, it's Abel. I don't suppose he'd be too hard to track down."

They arrived at Pizza Hut and settled at a small table for two. The red vinyl tablecloth had a nick out of it where fluffy backing tufted through. Alice watched a little kid playing with a pizza man puppet. She rested her head on her elbows. There was a lot on her mind.

"Alice," said Chris. "Thanks for coming out with me."

"Thanks for asking."

"I didn't think you would, after the funeral and all this."

"Trust me, I needed this. Everyone else makes me feel like I'm crazy."

"Irv was going to ask you out," said Chris, "but I talked him out of it."

They placed an order, and Alice stirred her iced tea with her straw.

"So," said Chris, "what're you going to do? Now that you know?"

"Not much I can do. If the Smalleys are gone, it's over for Junior. I'll leave at the end of the school year. I don't want to be here."

"Because of the dogs?"

"Because of the way people act about the dogs. And the kids. I've been trying to get Junior help all year, and Sturgeon won't let me. Even before this problem took a"—Alice thought about how to put it—"a unique twist, people have been weird about everything. No one takes care of any trouble. Well, not you. At least you care about the strays."

"I'm a vet. It's what I do."

"Yeah, but you know what they are."

"Even weredogs do better when they're not strays." Chris sipped his soda.

"So, what's Mary?"

"Alice," said Chris. "I won't help you there. Mary's a friend and I respect her privacy."

"She's a person," said Alice. "I knew it."

"Mary's story isn't mine to tell," said Chris. "If it's any help, she's been helping round up the strays."

The evening loosened up. Alice asked about Chris and college. He'd met Irv and Mary at Iowa State, and Irv had suggested that the county would benefit from a vet practice, so it was a great opportunity for Chris. Alice told Chris that she'd become a teacher because her mother, her hero, was a teacher, and there was never any question about following in Mom's footsteps.

After pizza they ended up at the Richley Tap. Over an hour-glass-shaped mug of Pabst, Alice answered Chris' last question. "It's true. Teachers aren't allowed to drink in their own town. We could, but it is 'frowned upon'. When I lived above the bar, I took the outside staircase down."

Chris swirled his Coke and ice. "How do teachers feel about things like, well, other licentious activities?"

Alice gulped her beer. "I can't speak for Thelma Schwartz, but I'm all for it."

An autumn wind was kicking up the dust on the street as they left the bar. Leaves glided down from the trees. Chris held the Charger door open for her. They took back roads home, and they detoured into a scenic view. The moon, full and bright, was a jewel in a mystic blue sky. Below the hill a pond rippled its reflection.

Alice opened the door. She wanted to slip her shoes and hose off and run in the grass, climb the fence, and swim in the pond, but the people in the nearby house might not like that. The lights were out. Maybe they weren't home.

Chris draped her coat across her shoulders and left his hands there. She sank back into him. "I had fun," Alice said.

"Me too," said Chris. "Let's do this again. We might go as far as Des Moines next time."

Alice turned toward him and stepped in. His lips were firm when she kissed him. It was a first date kiss, each person getting the measure of attraction, the texture of the lips, the correct tilt of the head. Alice smoothed stray hair into his part. "Okay," said Alice. "Des Moines."

He kissed her again. Alice's coat puddled on the ground. The kiss lasted longer this time. Alice pressed her body against him. His muscles were chiseled, but her body flowed around them, fitting into his dips and curves. His lips sought her neck, which pushed little pins into the back of her knees.

"Chris," she said, speaking into his hair.

His reply was airy and muffled.

"Stop."

He straightened. "Really?" He nipped her ear.

"Mmm," she said. Pleasure tingled down her neck and across her shoulders. "Really. Someone's coming."

The ambulance almost ran them off the road, sirens squalling, as it sped by. A pickup rambuckled toward them, three men in the back holding rifles. Bill Halcomb was driving.

"Hey Doc," said one of the men. "We need you."

"What happened?" asked Alice.

Bill Halcomb leaned out the window. "Car accident, Miss Brubaker. Ambulance is seeing to the crash. A steer's been torn up, too."

"I'm on it," said Chris.

Alice sat down in the Charger. They followed as the pickup turned onto a gravel road. Over the next hill, Alice saw pillars of light glowing into the sky. A mangled car lay at the bottom of a ravine, propped over a dead tree so that the headlights goggled upwards. The taillights winked provocative pools of red onto the ground.

The road had no shoulder. Parked as close to the edge of the road as possible, the ambulance made the scene look like a grotesque Christmas. On the ground nearby, a steer bellowed in panic.

"Hit by the car," said Halcomb. His jaw set and he took a rifle from the back seat. "Take a look, Doc."

Alice climbed out of the truck and looked into the ravine, sweat cooling her body. Irv clanked out of the back of the ambulance, pulling a stretcher. "What're you doing out here, Alice?"

"Bill stopped and asked Chris about the cattle." The smell of blood was overpowering, no doubt the damaged steer. "Who was in the car?"

"Patrice Smalley."

They weren't gone. Where had she been? Alice squinted, as if that would help her see through the dark. "How is she?"

"She's dead, Alice. Go back to the car," Irv said. "You don't need to be here."

Alice walked to the edge of the ravine and looked down. At her feet was a dog, crushed by a car, a young dog, small. She jumped back, her stomach flip-flopping.

"You're sure?" Halcomb asked behind her.

"It'd be humane," said Chris.

Halcomb pulled the trigger. A bullet echoed through the air and the panicked steer was silent.

———•••———

Oscar Springs came out for the second funeral in two weeks. Loathed in life, Patrice Smalley became a martyr in death. The town was abuzz with speculation. She worked nights out at the plastic factory over in Creston. The theory was that she'd fallen asleep at the wheel, and she'd seen the steer too late, swerved and driven off the road. The back end of the car was pancaked, and Patrice's body was shredded going through the windshield on the way down. It was a closed casket funeral. The church was filled to capacity. As with Mark Halcomb's funeral, folding chairs had to be set up in the basement.

The town undercurrent of gossip speculated about where the family had been, some saying they'd cleared out during Halcomb's funeral, others suggesting that Abel had drank all their moving money, so they had to move back. Abel Smalley reappeared in public. He was so shocked about his wife's death that he didn't drink for four days. He shaved and put on an ancient suit and narrow black tie from the sixties. Junior, who turned out to not be in juvenile detention, sleepwalked through life. He left the funeral halfway through the sermon. Afterwards he was found outside, sitting on the church's handicapped ramp with his head in his hands. When Alice returned home from school at night, she saw him leaning against the paint-chipped house, watching the road. The smart as a whip sister did not materialize.

Like he hadn't been gone, Junior came back to school after a week, although his attendance was sporadic. His clothes became shabbier, and his appearance became more unkempt. Kids teased him about cooties and stinking. Alice suggested to the gym teacher that he let Junior shower after PE, but since that wasn't standard elementary practice, Sturgeon was inflexible.

The Smalleys no longer had an income and there was no money for Junior. When Junior brought a plastic bag of baking coconut for lunch one day, the staff began to collect money for his meals.

Mary was under the weather. Each night she had circled the house, but she stopped. She hid under the crawl space, where she slept for long periods of time, her paws over her nose. When she didn't, she stared across the street at the Smalley's dilapidated house. Chris looked her over and gave her a clean bill of health. Irv took her home.

One night, while Melody was staying out at Tim's, Alice came home late from school to find Junior sitting on their porch. She froze. Junior was grubby, his hair greasy, wearing jeans with frayed patches.

"Junior?"

Junior stood up. "I wanted to see your dog," Junior said. "Where is she?"

"Gone," said Alice.

"She's a nice dog," said Junior.

"Yes, she is." Alice cast about for what to say next, and the words popped out. "Have you and your dad had any trouble with the strays?"

"That won't be happening no more," said Junior, like he knew. "You sure your dog is gone?"

"She wasn't mine. She's gone home."

There was a pivot, as though Junior was weighing how to react to that intelligence. Alice watched him pause. Junior sank down, folding in on himself. Tears cut dirty paths down his face. Alice took a deep breath. She sat down beside him and spoke like she would to a spooked animal. "Junior?"

When Junior took a good look at her after sobbing for a few minutes, he found himself sitting by her on the porch. He shot up and walked away, like he had been caught stealing.

"Junior?" Alice stepped beside him. "Have you eaten?"

"No."

"Come in," said Alice. "Come inside."

"I don't want to."

"Wait here. Let me get you a sandwich. Promise me you'll

wait here."

Alice didn't stop to make it. She grabbed bread, peanut butter and a knife from the kitchen, and let the screen door slam on its spring before the kid had time to change his mind. She slathered the white bread in peanut butter, and Junior wolfed slice after slice of it.

She returned to the kitchen and came back with a glass of milk. Junior gulped it and wiped his mouth on his arm. After he was done, he walked back across the street.

"Enough" said Alice, watching him go. "That's enough."

⬥⬥⬥

Alice sat across from Sturgeon. His face looked like a wall did after a flood, faded stains of previous anger covered with the red stains of current anger. His voice filled the office, bounced off the window, and bludgeoned Alice's eardrums. "I was called by channel nine news! Channel nine news! They wanted to know about the Smalleys, and they said you had called them because we wouldn't call in Junior's case as abuse."

Alice shifted on the edge of her seat. She wanted to wrap her hands around Sturgeon's neck. "If you saw—"

Sturgeon dropped his arms to the desk and leaned toward her, his face purpling. He looked like an angry ape. "We were handling matters internally."

"No," said Alice. "You weren't. It's over now. Junior's going to get the help he needs and that's for the best."

"Miss Brubaker, you are suspended, pending further investigation into this matter."

"I don't think you can do that," Alice said. She fought to keep her voice even, felt her own cheeks color with emotion, her ears hot. She imagined punching Sturgeon in the face. "While the board could make that decision, the union would make sure you lost that battle. You don't want more bad press, and if you suspended me, I'd make sure there was more."

Sturgeon sputtered as he tried to form words. "Get out!"

Alice left the office. Erlene snubbed her by pretending to be busy with a notebook. Alice walked into the sparsely populated after school hallway. *Jerk! Jerk! Jerk!*

The last thing Alice had on her list before she left for home was getting the Halloween decorations out of the basement so the kids could put them up tomorrow. She headed downstairs to the ground floor. The concrete walls had been divided into two colors--a cerulean blue covered the bottom and a robin's egg shade climbed all the way to the high ceiling. The painters had become less cautious as they had moved underground. Drips and rivulets were braille bumps on the wall as she descended to the basement level.

Alice passed the janitor's office. "Larry?" Through the half-opened door, she could see the boiler, which looked like a cross between a submarine and an octopus. She waited. No one was there. Fine. She'd be fast, and there'd be no trouble. Just in and out. She wouldn't breathe any asbestos. Then she'd go for a run, bleed off some of her anger. Hopefully her feet wouldn't give her any grief.

She wandered down the ramp past the radiator and stopped at the door to the storage area. Alice fiddled with her key but discovered that the door was open. She jutted out her lower lip and blew out a puff of air that fluttered her bangs upward. She went in.

Boxes of holiday decorations were heaped in a festive labyrinth, glittery tinsel peeking out of one box, a long Christmas tree box held together by dusty masking tape. She hoped she could locate the scarecrows and pumpkins among the mad mountains of Easter and Christmas crammed away in haste. Alice moved toward the fifth-grade pile, and that's when she heard the crying.

It was a cross between an animal whimper and a sob. There was a sort of vocalization, a whine that sounded like when trainers on television try to take credit for a dog speaking words. Alice paused and stepped backwards. Then she shook her head. If there was a kid in here, hurt, she was a teacher and that was all there was to it. "Hello?"

The whimpering echoed and spiraled, intensifying. Alice squared her shoulders and flipped on the light. The naked ceiling bulb above the boxes glowed. There was running, movement behind a box. A bloody handprint marred cardboard. Alice's moved the box, and her eyes followed the whimper to the floor.

The body was a boy's except that the forearms had shortened, and fingers shrank back into paws. The face was also in transition, jaw jutted out in a snout, his nose and lip elongating away from his face.

Later, Alice was ashamed she ran. At the time, she couldn't imagine doing anything else, her heart pounding in her throat, the pounding filling her ears. She was two blocks away from the school, almost down to the railroad tracks, when she stopped, her blood singing in her ears. Taking several deep breaths, she marched back to the school, found Larry in the boiler room, and took him into the storage room with her. There was nothing there, and she let Larry think she had seen a mouse. Let him laugh.

She had enough wherewithal to grab the fifth-grade decorations for Halloween. The bloody handprint was still on the cardboard. It looked like red tempura paint.

———•••———

"Fuck," Alice said to no one. She sat in the easy chair, staring at the television's blank screen. Melody was sleeping over at Tim's again. Alice tried to wrap her mind around storage rooms and dog children. The room grew darker as she sat in the chair. She sipped beer from a glass bottle.

She hadn't recognized the dog boy, but it could have been any child. Who would be gone from school tomorrow? The chickenpox kids. Was the boy one of the sick kids? No one was missing them. Every kid she sent to the office, now that she thought about it, those were the kids who got sick.

Alice walked into the kitchen and rinsed her face with water. Was she going mad? Too much stress?

No. She had seen the boy-dog. Why in Heaven's name would her brain make that up? She knew the truth. Chris knew the truth. Of course, in order to be a weredog, someone would have to change. It looked ghastly, painful.

Her life was now like a bad drive-in film. Being in a bad drive-in movie was unacceptable. Before, it was only words, a theory in the air. Now it was living children with stretching bone and sinew. Dead boys with scars, whose bodies ripped as they transformed, scars arranged neatly by whom? A paramedic? A veterinarian? Alice paced the kitchen. She paced a little more. She had to trust someone. She dialed Chris' number. He was on his way over in seconds.

The knocking startled her. She went right to the door. Abel Smalley stood outside. Since Patrice's death, Abel Smalley had shrunk into himself even more, his eyes empty and glittering. The shadows of the evening pooled into the hollows of his eyes and cheekbones. She wanted to shake him like a terrier holding onto a rat. *How dare you starve your son! How dare you!*

"Where's my boy?" slurred Abel Smalley.

Her voice shook as she replied. "This is a really bad time, Abel." Was he going to try to bite her? She wanted that shotgun next to her bed. She wanted bullets, not rock salt.

"Where's my son, you goddamned bitch! He at that school?"

"Now you listen to me! You get out of here right now!" She shook, but she wasn't going to back down.

Abel tried to push his way into the room, but Alice held the door against him, letting the bottle tumble to the floor, sticky liquid coating her ankle.

"You and Sturgeon," Abel yelled. "You want Junior, but he's my son! Belongs to me! He's mine!"

"Abel!" A sharp, angry bellow from an angry man, cracking like a clap of thunder.

Smalley let the door go slack. "You! I'll goddamn fucking kill you!" Abel disappeared.

Alice stepped outside. Chris stood there, his face contorted like some avenging Greek god. "Get out of here! Go!"

Abel launched himself at Chris, and as he did so, he changed, his body sliding from drunken human to mangy dog. It was easier than it had been with the little boy, a fluid change like an arc of water from a garden hose. Alice felt reality was slipping on a newly waxed floor. Then reality rounded the corner as Chris changed too. He grew at least two feet, becoming something between man and dog, long arms and claws and teeth. He caught Abel and launched him over his head, into the trunk of a tree. Abel yelped, and Alice heard a wet smack. Abel skittered back toward his house.

Chris shifted into the largest dog Alice had ever seen. No, not a dog. A gray wolf that turned his head as he looked at her with Chris' blue eyes. Chris pursued Abel across the street. Alice ran back into the house. Shredded clothes littered Alice's lawn.

Her hands trembled as she dialed Irv's phone number. She had to try it three times before she dialed right. She left an incomprehensible message on his answering machine, ripped through phone book pages trying to find out how to contact the Ripley fire department, and left a message for him there.

Maybe you don't want to get involved with Chris. Irv's voice inside her head. Alice pulled the bead curtain back and glanced outside. She couldn't see the wolf and the dog, but she could hear snarls and rending metal from across the street. She went back in the kitchen and eyed the knives in the cutting block. Yeah, like one of those would be helpful. She sank down to the floor by the sticky beer puddle and put her hands over her ears. It didn't keep the noise out, but it reduced it to a garbled crunching.

She couldn't stand it. She opened the door. She couldn't see anything.

A siren made her jump. The ambulance pulled up and Irv climbed out of the front seat. Mary jumped through the window and raced for Smalley's, growling, hot on a scent.

"Alice!" Irv grabbed her, pulled her close, and she sank into him, letting some of the fear bleed out of her. "Are you okay?"

"Chris! He's over there! He's—"

"Not from around here. Yeah." Irv pushed her back. "Are you hurt?" His professional eye wandered up and down her, from the top of her cloudy head to her stocking feet.

"No. I'm not. Irv, what the Hell is going on?"

"I gotta get over there right now."

"No, you don't," said Alice. "You're going to tell me what's going on here. What's going on with Chris? And those kids?"

"Kids?"

She clamped on to his arm.

He pulled his arm away. "Not now, Alice. Life and death. Paramedic, remember?"

"I swear, Irv. I'll do something drastic." What, she didn't

know. She felt like her head might explode.

"Stay right here," said Irv. "Stay right here."

Irv raced across the street. A yelp cut short echoed back toward them.

"Irv?" Alice swallowed. She ran back into the house, slid on her sneakers and followed, wondering why the hell she would do that.

At the Smalley home, there were three of them. Mary squared off against the dog that was Abel Smalley. He sunk his teeth into her leg, and she yelped. She scrabbled, but Abel pulled her in and lunged with sharp fangs for her throat. The gray wolf was back to being the monster, and Chris balanced a ripped piece of steel from one of the mechanics ramps and swung it at Abel. The jagged edge sliced Abel's head off, sending it flying across the yard into high grass.

The trembling female shrank, blinking into a slender woman standing near one of the dead cars. Irv draped his large jacket over her, her bare legs reflecting the last of the sun.

Chris, instantly nude, was on all fours. Irv pulled out a first aid kit and started patching up gashes along his side, those that weren't closing themselves. Alice headed toward the woman.

"Don't," Chris croaked.

Irv looked up. "Alice, you freeze. You stay right where you are. Mary, go find his head."

Mary. A weredog. Of course. Alice swallowed. She didn't feel good about having been right.

Mary turned toward Alice, her large brown eyes the same brown eyes as before. "No," she said, her voice shaky. "Not yet."

"Alice," said Irv. "Go get Chris a blanket from the ambulance."

Alice stood her ground.

"You do it," said Irv, firm and insistent.

Alice walked through the motions and handed Irv a fire blanket. Irv handed it to Chris. Chris stood without a scratch on him, looking like he had just left the shower.

"What will you tell the county?" Mary asked.

"That the ramp rusted through and the car on top crushed him. Old metal sliced his head off." Chris looked at Irv, and he nodded approval. "We should go."

"No," said Alice. "No one goes anywhere, until I know what's going on. Chris, what the Hell was that?"

"I'm not a dog," said Chris. "I'm a wolf. My kind, we make it our business when a pack gets out of control and starts killing, or humans get out of control and start killing us."

"You could have told me that the other night," said Alice.

"Not the kind of information you drop on a potential girlfriend at Pizza Hut after she's just figured out that the dogs in town aren't dogs. Believe me, this isn't the way I wanted you to find out."

"You killed him," Alice said. "You killed Abel Smalley."

"Yes," said Chris.

Alice couldn't read those frank blue eyes. Could she live with it, that he'd killed Abel Smalley?

"I wanted to kill him," said Mary. "Dad was going to hurt me again." Mary spread her hands to encompass the junky yard. "I wanted to rip his head off, put an end to him." Mary pulled up one of Irv's gigantic sleeves to show her arm. Alice saw the dark shadow of blood. "He used to--"

Irv shook his head and put an arm around Mary's shoulders. "You don't have to tell Alice anything, Mary."

"No, it's okay, Irv. He used to cut me when he was angry. And of course, I'd heal up. Slice me to ribbons, leave me in the ditch, let me heal up, do it again. Mom knew. She didn't do anything. He had a silver knife he threatened to use. If he'd sliced me with the silver, he would have killed me. I ran as soon as I could."

Dad? Alice heard the words like a slap in the face. "And you left your brother with him?"

Mary hung her head. "I'm back now." She stared at Alice. "I'll do what's right now."

"Can Junior–does Junior change like you?"

"No. Me and Dad, we change our shape," said Mary. "Junior can't. Patrice is my stepmom. Because she isn't one of us, Junior's normal, like she was."

"Junior's not normal." said Alice. "I don't think you're right. Junior bit Mark Halcomb. Mark died because he changed. His bite makes people change."

"Junior can't do that," said Mary.

"You don't know," said Irv. "Your dad could have put him up to it."

"No," said Mary. "He can't. Even if he could, he hates Dad. We both do."

"No offense," said Irv, "but you were away a long time. You don't know Junior."

"You need to know—" said Alice.

"I know my brother better than you do," said Mary.

"Stop!" yelled Alice. "Stop!" She massaged her temples and found her compass while the rest of them stared at her. "There's some kids gone from school. Chickenpox they said. Today, I saw a dog—a boy—a dog-boy in the storeroom. That's why I called Chris. Something is going on at the school. Kids go away. Some come back. Maybe some don't. Junior's biting kids to make dogs," said Alice. "Your dad is putting him up to it."

"You cold bastards. You assume Junior would do this."

"Maybe Junior's making his own pack?" said Irv.

"That's not the way this works," said Chris. "Junior can't

become a weredog. He can't make weredogs."

"You think Abel?" asked Irv.

"No. I'll be damned if I know who," said Chris, "but I want to find out. I think we need to go to the school."

"You shouldn't have come," said Irv.

"It's my school," said Alice. "What kind of teacher would I be if I stayed at home? Besides, you need me. I'm the native guide, and I have the key. You don't change into anything weird, and you're here. Do you?"

Irv shined the flashlight on the lock. "Don't be stupid."

"Well, why would you tell me?"

Mary sniffed the air and barked.

Chris held up a hand. "There's been a transformation here recently. Mary and I can smell it." He knelt by Mary. "Follow your nose."

Alice unlocked the school. Downstairs, the smell of stale heating oil was overwhelming. Chris knelt by a handprint on the floor, like the one on the side of the Halloween box. "That handprint's not paint."

Mary turned and headed back toward the boiler room. Dust clogged the air. "Why's this area shut off?" asked Irv.

"Asbestos removal. We're not supposed to be down here until it's taken out at Christmas."

The door to the boiler room was locked. Irv looked at Alice. "No," Alice sighed. "I don't have a key for that."

Chris squeezed the handle and twisted. Metal twisted and the door popped.

The barking inside exploded.

Dogs and children lined the walls, sleeping in huddles. Some of the kids had been missing from class, others attended every day. In the center of the room were four cages. Two of them held restless dogs. Joel and Tom, still boys, were in the other cages. Joel had a bandage around one arm. Tom, dazed, sat slumped in a corner. Joel covered his eyes with his hands to avoid the brightness from the flashlight. As he blinked, he spoke. "Please," he said. "Please help me!"

A couple of the human children laughed, older boys from the third floor. Alice stared at the kids with what they might call the stink eye, and they shut up. The dogs, however, shook themselves awake. Mary growled at them.

"Joel, where are the keys?" Alice kept her voice calm and reassuring. She couldn't help but notice that the dogs were circling under the direction of the older kids.

"I don't know."

"You aren't supposed to be here," said one of the teenagers. He began to shift, not the jerky horrible movements of the boy in the storeroom, but not the blink of an eye that it took Abel Smalley.

Chris flared into a giant mountain of wolf. The teen stepped away, yelping, his tail between his shortening legs. The dogs cowered, covering their noses. Joel screamed. Alice screamed.

Chris picked up the boy by the scruff of his neck. "Who's responsible for this?" His teeth glistened. "Abel Smalley?"

The teenage dog wet himself.

"Who did this?"

"He bit me," Joel managed to say. "He bit me.

Alice shook her head. "Why don't their parents know they're gone?" asked Alice, her mind flailing for the normal. "Why wouldn't anyone know they're missing?" Some of them weren't missing, she realized. They were already dogs. The chickenpox was an excuse to get a few more, Alice realized, from the most difficult kids whose parents weren't paying attention.

Tom whimpered and his transformation began. The boy's

mouth and nose stretched, and his body twisted. Irv's flash-light made him into a grotesque shadow puppet. When Alice was a girl watching *Pinnochio*, she remembered the boys turning into donkeys on Pleasure Island. That part had scared her so much she had to sleep with her parents. She wanted to look away, but with a teacher's duty, she stood riveted to the spot and watched. Tom's ears stretched and folded in half. The boy howled. The dogs whined.

Joel backed further into a corner. "No," he said, "I don't want that to happen to me."

"Of course." Alice looked at Irv. "You all knew about the Smalleys and Mary. The town turns a blind eye."

"Yeah, well." Irv watched the circle of dogs. "With Abel it was a few of his drunken buddies. You're right, Mary. This can't be Junior."

"Thank you," said Mary, changing back into herself.

"Yeah, well. I'm sorry." Irv covered her with his jacket again, staying close. "Kids don't think like this. Abel doesn't either. It's got to be someone else."

"We call the police, right?" Alice asked. "This is kidnapping, child endangerment."

"Yeah," said Irv. "Okay. Not Kimball, though. He's useless."

Chris had stared the circle of dogs and children into submission. Without looking away, he spoke, his voice thick. "Mary, take Alice home. Call the sheriff in Richley, Alice."

"What about you and Mary? They'll know."

"Don't really care," said Chris. "The important thing is to take care of these kids. Irv, we need to get some things from the clinic. Or the ambulance. Depends on the kid."

How dare someone do this to her students? Who? "Someone at the school has to be responsible." She thought Larry. Who else would have access to the boiler room? Who else could set up the asbestos lie?

"One thing at a time, Alice. We'll get there. You and Mary, be careful."

Alice stepped out into the cool night. She ran down the road toward her house, Mary hot on her heels. A car pulled away from the school, and a green Buick pulled alongside her, one she recognized, one she saw every day. Mr. Sturgeon.

"Miss Brubaker?" Sturgeon rolled down the window. "Did you just come out of the school?"

"Yes," she said. *Keep it cool, Alice.*

"You know you're required to sign in at the office for late night visits. I was up there, and you didn't stop in."

He was being an officious bastard, and she didn't have time for it. "I'm sorry," she said. "I went in to drop off some assignments. I'll make sure to sign in next time."

Mary growled. Alice studied the darkness by the side of the road. *Please let it be a cat, or a squirrel, or even an ordinary dog.* A snarl issued from the shadows and a furry bullet shot onto Mary. Mary rolled with the dog over the gravel and into the ditch grass. Alice turned away from the car just in time for the driver's side Buick door to catch her full in the back. She pitched forward, scratching hands and legs on the gravel, her skin shredding. Sturgeon grabbed fistfuls of her dress, jerked open one of the back doors, and tumbled her into the backseat. She tried to get back out, but he hit her in the stomach. The air burst out of her, and she couldn't breathe. Then Sturgeon punched her in the face. A tooth chipped.

Something hard hit her on the head, and stickiness, blood, ran down her face. Her head stung and she covered it with her hands. Sturgeon pushed her legs in the car.

The car skidded down the road. Alice didn't pass out, but she couldn't do much as her consciousness flickered like the streetlight outside her house.

———◆•◆———

Alice's consciousness danced like campfire flames around the fringes of what she thought must be her concussion. She sweated, and her stomach did gymnastics.

Sturgeon. Why Sturgeon? It didn't make any sense. But it did. How could you hide something like children in the basement from the building principal? Asbestos her eye.

She wasn't alone in the back seat. Junior was there, breathing fast and shallow. The boy was terrified. Sturgeon pulled up at a barn. "Get out!" Sturgeon barked at Junior. "And stay the hell out of my way."

Junior scurried out of the car toward the building.

"You see what it gets you," said Sturgeon to Alice. "You see what it gets you. You should have left it alone, Alice. You should have left me alone." He plucked her out of the car, carrying her over one shoulder, treating her like a side of beef more than a human being.

"Who are you?"

"An outsider. Like you. When I first came to Oscar Springs, I had your idealism. You don't have to be here long before you change. You just damned well wouldn't change." Alice caught the pinpricks of eyes reflecting the car headlights. Fewer dogs here, in the country, maybe five or six. Sturgeon took her inside the spare, gray barn. She threw up where Sturgeon threw her in the corner, her mouth bitter with the taste.

Stupid. Chris had sent Mary as a bodyguard, but Alice had stumbled into Sturgeon like an idiot. She was boiling inside, angry at herself, at Sturgeon. Alice struggled to sit up and waves of dizziness drowned her. "Those children," she said. "Why?"

"Abel Smalley bit me. At first, he had the run of me, the rest of the pack higher than me in the pecking order. I got damned sick of it, and we had it out. I became the leader, which isn't hard in a pack where the other dogs drink themselves into oblivion. Abel's damned friends.

"I didn't want a pack full of pathetic drunk men. I wanted my own pack." Sturgeon took off his shoes, which Alice thought peculiar since the barn floor was dirt. "My own. At first, I recruited from the third floor. Delinquents, the kind of kids that wouldn't let their parents give them any grief." Sturgeon loosened his tie. "We were becoming a strong pack, but we had problems. The older kids, they question authority. Children, now, you raise a child, they do what you tell them to. You use children from the parents who don't care, or who want to be turned themselves."

Sturgeon unbuttoned his shirt. "People here are sheep," he said. "Every once in a while, Abel thinks he's gotta show me he's boss. Keeping Junior close usually keeps him in line, but he's a drunk."

"Junior bites children. He doesn't turn them?"

"Jesus, Alice, no. Junior bites kids all right and cuts up kitties, because that's how his old man solves his problems. Junior's a troubled boy, just like you thought. He needs help. Too bad he can't have it.

"I bit Mark first and told Junior to bite him. It makes the boy feel powerful and I was sick and tired of those damn farmers killing my pack. Halcomb's their leader, and he's a pain in my ass. I wanted some leverage.

"Abel messed things up. Abel cut Mark up with a silver knife and I lost him to you. What a mess. You almost cost me everything there, Alice. Mark would have healed up after a time, and he would have told everyone about me, but he decided to run home to Daddy who shot him. That was damned lucky. Of course, Abel'd take that blame as far as Bill Halcomb was concerned.

"I killed Patrice to remind Abel who was in charge now. You were too damned interested in Junior and too smart, putting it all together. You were out of control.

"You messed it all up, didn't you? You wouldn't take a hint. Calling the AEA, calling the news, trying to save this boy, finding out too much. Congratulations." Sturgeon clapped. "Don't worry, Alice. I'll give you the reward you deserve. We're going to play a game. I can't tell you how much I am going to enjoy this. If you can beat me, I'll let you live. Pack could use some bitches, and you're one pretty strong-willed bitch, aren't you?

"If you can't outrun me, I'll eat you. Which is pretty much what you damned well deserve." He prodded her with a foot. "Can you even run? I like my prey to have a little sport in them. Come on," he prodded her again, "get up. Get going. I'll give you a head start." He shimmied out of his pants, and he began to change into a giant covered with fur.

"You're not a dog."

"I am. But I'm more. I'm the leader, and I can draw on the whole pack for strength. No one but the alpha can become this." He stood in front of her, a giant canine monster, his jaws dripping.

Alice shook her head. She hooked spaces in the slats of the wall with her fingers to climb her way upright.

Junior, from somewhere out of her vision, appeared in front of her.

"Is that how we're playing this?" Sturgeon said, his voice full of teeth and saliva.

"It's not right," said Junior. "I won't let you."

"Don't get in my way, or I'll kill you."

"You won't kill me. You need me."

"Bad boys deserve to be punished. You know from your father that we can't always control ourselves, don't you?"

"Run away," Alice said to Junior.

Junior ignored her.

"I'm coming, Alice, after I count to thirty. Get going."

Junior dragged Alice, stumbling, outside. Around the barn, the glassy eyes of a circle of dogs set up the perimeter. Young dogs, in-town strays, fighting and snarling over cuts of meat that had been left to feed them. Dogs who could be trained to obey, who could become wild dogs with the snap of Sturgeon's fingers. Blood on their maws.

Her students.

"Come on," said Junior.

"The car," said Alice. Sturgeon could outrun them. He might not be able to break into the car right away.

Junior trundled her into the back seat and plunged the locks down. He grabbed a rifle, the butt of it covered with hair and blood. Hers. He pulled something out of his waistband. "Take it," he said. Alice pulled a knife out of its sheath. The blade was silver.

"Dad's," said Junior.

A dog leaped onto the hood of the car and barked, slavering white teeth gleaming in gray moonlight. Alice crammed the knife into a skirt pocket. Through the windshield, she watched Sturgeon bound out of the barn, a fury machine. One dog challenged him. Sturgeon scooped up the dog, broke its neck, and slung it aside like a rag. The other dogs backed away. Sturgeon sniffed the air. "I should have treated you more gently. You'd be a better hunt." His red eyes gazed right at the car, and he picked it up and threw it.

Alice's stomach was empty, but she heaved as she and Junior tumbled about the car like ball bearings. Junior's body struck her hard as he was thrown into her. The car landed on its side and rolled twice, the glass of the windows crunching underneath. More blood, although she didn't know if it was hers or Junior's.

"Junior?" She couldn't see him. Had he been thrown from the car? Where had he gone? She groped and found the rifle. The knife was still with her, her hand pressing it to her thigh through the skirt like her life depended on it. It probably did.

Sturgeon peeled the side of the car away like the top of a sardine can. The metal squealed and he threw it aside. His giant silhouette stood out against the moon and stars. He pulled back his head and howled. The dogs in the pack howled in response. The pit of Alice's stomach filled with acid and panic. He was going to gut her like a deer, he was going to sink his claws into her throat, and then, then he was going to devour her. Adrenaline overtook panic and she emptied the rifle into the silhouette, the shot jarring against her shoulder bringing on new waves of double vision.

Sturgeon doubled over and felt his midsection, the surging of blood there. He laughed and straightened, grabbing her wrist and dangling her by one arm as he lifted her up to his eyes. The pack of dogs barked closer. His jaws separated, saliva streaming. His teeth sank into her shoulder.

And then a freight train hit Sturgeon. Alice felt the claws of another monster. She was thrown away, landing hard on the ground. She watched Chris and Sturgeon rip into each other, the noise like two demons fighting, savage and angry cries, guttural howling, the ripping of flesh and fur, the smack of muscle on bone.

There were hands on her, and she winced. "No, it's me." Irv. "It's okay. I've got you. You're safe."

"Junior?"

"He'll live."

"It's Sturgeon," said Alice.

"Christ," Irv swore, looking at her mangled shoulder. "Did

Chris bite you?"

Alice was woozy. She placed her hand on her shoulder, felt the stickiness there. "No. The other one." She was aware of a burning sensation near her thigh. Silver. Weredogs. She'd think about that later. She needed to help Chris.

Sturgeon and Chris grappled. One monster reached into the mouth of the other and pulled the jaws apart, and there was a loud snap of dislocation.

"Chris!"

Sturgeon backhanded Chris, and the wolf flew into the rubble of the car, impaled on jagged metal. Sturgeon's jaw dangled loose as he made his way toward Irv and Alice. Irv shot at Sturgeon, who kept coming forward. "God damned dogs!" Irv shouted.

Sturgeon picked Irv up by the head, shook him, and threw him aside into the stubble of harvested corn. He grabbed Alice around the neck and squeezed his claws into her throat. Blood slicked the fur of his paw.

Anger exploded inside of Alice. Her body tingled and shifted. She plunged the silver knife into Sturgeon's chest. He dropped her, and Alice let momentum carry her down his torso, the blade gliding through his flesh. Sturgeon growled and clamped her head. She flicked the knife upwards, and he howled, dropping her again.

A large piece of metal emerged from Sturgeon's chest as Chris impaled Sturgeon with the car's driveshaft. Sturgeon fell to the ground and Alice crawled forward. Under the driveshaft, Alice saw what remained of Sturgeon's heart, rent by claws and metal. Alice used the knife to cut it out. After all, Sturgeon had been pretty heartless and now reality matched what she already knew.

The adrenaline faded, like a genie flowing back into its bottle.

She fell to her knees, a warmth and peace enveloping her.

Town gossip being what it was, the speculation at first was that Walt Sturgeon had run off with Char Tate, Joel's mom. He was a no-good bastard anyhow, and she was a slut. The town seemed to breathe a sigh of relief, and Alice found it more interesting what the town wasn't saying. Then Kimball McBride announced that Walt Sturgeon had been found dead in a field. Cause of death, he said was a heart attack, which in all its elements was essentially correct. Alice knew that Kimball had been quick to accept how Abel Smalley had died too, but Kimball was as adamant as the sheriff at the end of *To Kill a Mockingbird* about the deaths, and Alice respected him for that one thing, if nothing else.

Chris leaned against one of the poles of Alice's rickety porch. The weather was finally cooling into fall, but it wasn't cold enough yet to drive them inside. "Irv says you check out well as a person. I should probably look you over next time you change into something else. Of course, not much damage sticks around with our kind."

Alice shook her head. "Still not sure how I feel being one of your kind"

"It's not so bad, in spite of recent events."

Alice crossed her arms and sat down on the steps. She patted the steps next to her and he joined her. "What if I become like him?"

"You won't." Chris wrapped his arm around her shoulders. "There's more control than that."

"Sturgeon had no control."

"Abel and Sturgeon had problems to begin with. You're pretty even-handed."

"I still don't understand how you came to be involved in

all this."

"Mary and Irv. They met me at college. It didn't take Mary long to figure out what I was. We came to get Abel. We didn't know about Sturgeon."

"Why would those parents let Sturgeon take their children? Why didn't anyone stand up to him?"

Chris kissed the top of her head. "Strangely enough, someone did."

She smiled. "Can you do that? Isn't this like some kinky interspecies thing? You being a vet and me being a teacher?"

"No hope for us then?"

Alice leaned her head on his shoulder.

Mary, human Mary, crossed the street. For days, junk trucks and tow trucks had been emptying the Smalley yard of debris. Eventually, the house would be torn down.

"You're looking better," said Mary.

"I'm feeling better," said Alice.

"I'm sorry about that night, that I wasn't more help."

"No reason to be sorry. How's Junior?"

"He's...Junior. We're leaving Oscar Springs. He's going to have a fresh start, and we're going to get him some help." Her eyes dared Alice to say something.

"Good," said Alice.

"I want you to know I'm not my mom and dad. I know I can't do this alone."

"Good," said Alice. "I heard Irv say he'd be visiting a lot."

Mary blushed. "Yeah, I heard that too."

Mary walked back across the street. Alice glanced at her wristwatch. "Gotta flip those burgers. Irv can put away, what, six of them?"

Alice didn't like the spare look of the house now that Melody had moved out to the farm with Tim, all married and with town approval. By the time Alice headed out to the backyard,

Irv and Chris were sitting at the picnic table, talking.

"So," said Irv. "You're staying?"

"I've put a lot of money into this practice. Where else am I gonna find one this close to my pack's territory? I'm pretty sure I'm the only doctor around who can treat the special cases, which this town's going to have dozens of. We could use a doctor too. Or someone close to a doctor."

Irv leaned over and smelled the burgers on the platter. "Buns?"

Alice motioned with her head toward a bag. "Go easy on the onions." She put the platter on the table.

"What about you?" asked Irv. "You staying?"

"What about you?" Alice put lettuce on her plate.

"Yes." Irv put a circle of mustard on the bun. "Kind of ironic, since I've spent my whole life trying to get out of Oscar Springs and I keep coming back."

"What about Mary?"

"Yeah," said Chris. "I heard that you really do have a girlfriend named Mary now. Funny how weredog trauma can bring people closer together."

"You can shut up any time now."

"So," said Alice, "a long distance relationship?"

"We have these things called cars. You've heard of them? Now, what about you?"

"What do you think?" Mary smiled. "I'm out of here."

"What?" Chris leaned forward.

Irv let mustard flow onto the ground.

"You said—" Chris stood up.

"It's okay, boys. For the summer. Becoming a principal's gonna take some extra classes. Nights and summers."

"Oh," said Chris.

"It's like you and Irv. We need someone at the school who can deal with the special cases. Someone who understands their unique problems and can make them mind."

And Alice was that someone. Of course she would stay. Because they were her students, and they needed her to take care of them, protect them.

She sat down at the table and popped open a can of diet soda. Chris raised his Coke. Irv raised his beer. "To us," said Chris.

"To all of us," said Alice. "And to Oscar Springs."

Sometimes, one of our local animal shelters solicits material for a fund-raiser. Cat Emperor is a tribute to our cat Michael, who passed on in the 1990s. He was an ace.

Cat Emperor

Heavy are the ears which wear the crown.
Cat Emperor Michael, master of all the yard he surveys.
Is it not good to be the neighborhood tom?
Called a cat and a half by the vet,
Your rodent-shaped medal honors you as an ace.

At his Imperial Pleasure, Michael
Explores the drainpipes under the streets,
Hones glaive-like claws on the bark of trees,
Suns on his pleasure deck,
And defies the invaders of his kingdom.
Snakes, rabbits, moles
Meet a bloody end on the spear tips of his teeth,
And cats of other clans
Driven back to their own yards, or even indoors
Where the weaker ones simper, raised on kibble and cream.

He vigils on alone
Under the porch swing, in the bushes, atop branches.
Clear green eyes of Argus, lidless, sleepless.
A movement in the grass, and Michael claws down the tree
To confront the rodent below.

It is a mouse most unholy,
Its fur brushed against the nap,
Eyes beady and defiant,
Tail like a serpent,
This beast from the basement's underbelly.

Michael raises his paw and smashes it down.
The mouse dances away, squeaking its battle cry,
And turns again to hold its ground.
Michael stares in surprise, but does not pounce,
For the Emperor admires bravery.

But the belly of the Emperor rumbles.
Let this mouse make good his last stand.
He will play with this noble enemy, toss him into the air,
Draw out with ceremony the last moment when Michael
crunches his bones.
Oh noble cat toy!
You are honored!

The tails of the gods are question marks.
Even emperors are subject to fate's whims.
The sun is blotted out by the man of the house,
Who dares to ask the Emperor what he is doing,
And takes the capricious side of the mouse.
The Emperor is lifted, borne away
In the arms of embarrassment,
But his face is sly,
For he will soon return to the yard
Without an escort,
Once again to bend it to his will.

Crystal Vision *appeared in Rob Pierce and Sean Craven's magazine* Swill. *I orginally wrote the piece as part of a triptych at Viable Paradise, where I took the same prompt and made three kinds of stories from it.* Empress Dark, *the science fiction story, appears in my first collection,* The Devil's Wingman and Other Stories. Crystal Vision *is the horror version.*

Crystal Vision

My granddaughter sits on a soft wool blanket I spread out for her in the middle of the living room. She stares into the wall like she's trying to see through a window. She's watching nothing. She's uncommon quiet for a toddler. Her staring lasts long enough for me to finish my Bud. As I swig that last gulp out of the can, she snaps back to the present like a rubber band pulls her back to our house.

I am a young grandma. Rita had Tori when she was sixteen. The three of us did just fine. Tori waddles to me, her pudgy hand gummy with a coating of saliva and graham cracker crumbs. I wipe it off with a pink Kleenex after putting the empty on a coaster. She totters back to the blanket. I paint that goofy grandma grin on my face. My baby can do nothing wrong.

Really, it's more like Tori is my daughter than my granddaughter. Joe, my boyfriend, thinks I should buy Tori a little leather jacket to match mine. I think that is the idea of a total pothead. I like dressing her in bright colors, pink dresses and bright sleepers. She loves driving, just like me. Last spring, I bought a side car for my bike. It rides low to the ground, a smoky egg with a rod that attaches to my Harley. From inside Tori can see everything she wants through the tinted Plexiglas door. We never go on the highway, just on the paved county road behind our development when we ride. Safety is concern number one.

Tori's little hands try to pull my new beer off the coffee table. In the summer heat it's left a ring of sweat. "No honey," I say. "Not for you." My granddaughter doesn't drink. Tori's just experiencing the world the way little kids do, dragging everything to themselves. I empty the can, then stack it with the ones I've replaced in the box to move it out of her way. Six in there.

I pop a new can open. A six pack doesn't make much of a dent anymore, but I know my limit. I watch Tori over the can's rim. She falls on her diapered butt. "Good one, sweetie." I drain about half the can, bitter and fizzy.

There's Tori's spooky stare again. Me, Rita and Tori, we all have those spooky pale eyes, you know, the ones that are clear blue and don't look like any color almost. That makes Tori's space out more spooky. Of course, my eyes aren't freaky unless I'm looking in a mirror. Rita spooks me out in pictures all over the house.

Maybe when Tori's spacing out, she's talking to her mommy. I don't see any reason why we should be haunted. No one told Rita to get in that damned car.

I bet Tori has ADD. I read this article about how mothers that drink heavily during pregnancy make kids with ADD. Tori's eyes are flying saucers. That's another sign something's not right in her head. She can't stick with anything for more than a minute.

I crawl off the couch toward her. Her mouth opens, little teeth perfect in a delighted smile. We play with her cloth-covered string for a while. You pull it, and the crinkle sort of straightens out, and it tinkles out "Pop Goes the Weasel" which I sing along to, and which makes Tori wave her hands. I shake my bike keys at her. She's not interested. So I throw an episode of *Dora the Explorer* into the DVD player. She watches the picture, eyes opened like full moons.

I slug back another can while Tori's eyes unfocus. I wonder what her mom is putting in her head. Tori and I were fine. Nothing would've happened if Rita hadn't gotten all maternal. Tori knows I wouldn't hurt her. Her mommy can't poison her against me. I wonder if Tori's gonna need some extra help in school. She's just slow. Or not.

There's nothing wrong with Tori. She's a baby. All those welfare people in and out. I stayed clean and sober for them, one day at a time. I ran out of days is all. I tip my beer upside down. Empty. And I'm at my limit. Enough beer to relax, but not so much that I'd lose control or couldn't take care of Tori. I take care of my baby granddaughter. I take that responsibility seriously.

Tori's teetering across the shag toward the kitchen. I chase her and this excites her. She squeals gleefully and picks up the pace. Her tiny tennis shoes slap the linoleum. I catch her and swing her toward the tall ceiling, just shy of the fan. Her tummy's in front of my face, and I blow on her tummy, making raspberries. She giggles and babbles.

The idea hits me. I heft her onto my right hip. "Wanna go for a ride with Grandma?"

I open the door into the garage. My motorcycle is American, thank you very much, not some rice burner that will put one of my friends out of their job. Joe and I prefer Harleys. This one is new, which I don't like, but nothing lasts forever. I trundle Tori into the side car, and I close the little egg hatch. She's my little chick now, staring and staring at me with those freaky blue eyes, but I'm not going to think about that.

I rev the bike into action. We sputter out of the garage, down the slope of the driveway, out of the cul-de-sac and into the muggy summer evening. County Road 16, right behind our development, is where I do my driving. Not too many cops on County Road 16 to ask about my license. I love the way my hair ruffles around me. Helmets are for fascists.

A glance down at the side car shows me that Tori is sleeping. Finally. Rita has shut up and Tori is getting some rest. The bike wobbles a little, but I correct.

The rushing air is cool around us. I love it. We slope gently around the first bend. The cross is still by the side of the road. Its plastic flowers are fading and the cross itself looks dirty. I accelerate. We shoot down the road like a bee on No Doz. Now that Rita's not talking to Tori, she's lecturing me all over, how I can't take Tori on the bike, her colorless eyes flashing. Bullshit. Tori likes to ride. Tori is grandma's girl.

I hook the bike around curve number two, a little sharper, but I lean into it. The front wheel stutters a bit. My old bike was poetry in motion. I hypercorrect and weave across the center line. We pass a car. At first I think it's a cop, but I realize it's Rita, chasing me. I'd clean that cross and put out some fresh flowers if she wasn't such a bitchy nag all the time.

Rita's horn blares and I flip her the bird. I ramp up the bike. We are a rocket speeding into the setting sun. I feel Rita's eyes boring into me. She's behind me, yelling at me, slamming on the horn, telling me to stop. The noise pierces like a siren. I close my eyes to squeeze her out of my head. You stay dead and you shut up! You don't tailgate a motorcycle like some establishment pig.

At the next tight curve, the bike folds sideways underneath me. The sidecar bounces like a rubber ball on the concrete. I skid across the road like a rock skipping across a pond. Burning leather. Evaporating flesh. A solid slam into the silver guardrail. My skull caves; my eyes blur. The world fills flashing blue and red. Where did the trooper come from? He's a looker. I'm a mess.

The sidecar twists and spins to a halt in front of me. Blood slicks the tinted window, but I can see those little eyes staring at me. Rita's not talking to me anymore because she's too busy talking to her daughter. Maybe I was wrong. Maybe that's not a bad thing. Little girls like to be with their mommy.

Mountains of Green, *my Gamora story, appeared first in* The Mammoth Book of Dieselpunk, *where it is still available. I wrote this story with that publication in mind, but as it slowly evolved into an Atompunk story, I was sure it was going to go on the submission-go-round. Imagine my surprise when Sean Wallace bought it. I wrote the story in less than a week, parts of it also while attending a science fiction convention in Detroit.*

This story is an experiment in using what I know of Japan from my time there. It lacks the perspective of an insider in Japanese culture, but does have the perspective of someone who has thought a lot about what she has seen and experienced there. The lives of refugee children in post-World War Two Japan, and the changes Americans made to that country during the occupation have been well-documented, as has the Japanese reception to survivors of the bombings of Hiroshima and Nagasaki.

Mountains of Green

Kayo sharpened the corners of the sheet she folded into a perfect square, just so. Even though it was laundry to be done, Mrs. Sasa preferred the customer to have a neat impression of her service. Kayo folded, her eyes on bleached cotton. She did not look at him, although she felt him looking at her, his blue eyes skimming her smooth black hair like he was using his hands, caressing her ears, and touching her long braids. She kept her face as smooth as the white sheet.

She also felt the other set of eyes, like *kami* were watching her, in the distance, hovering over the scene. She wondered if the spirits of Japan liked the Occupation. The eyes of the *kami* watched her hands pluck a second sheet from the pile of dirty laundry, watched Private Quill and his *gaikokujin* face, pulled outside, looked down onto the converted city hall, now American barracks, and hovered over cars and bicycles in the narrow streets, the rubble and the makeshift buildings in the neighborhoods of Hakodate.

Quill said something to her in English and left. Kayo exhaled, slowed her breathing, unclenched. His footsteps faded away, and she turned toward Quill's desk. Quill always left presents for her. Today he had left her three things, and two were useful. There was half a bag of rice, much too dear for her to afford, and a chocolate bar, which she would not care for, but which she would pass along to her little brother Isao, who would sell chunks of it to the boys he played with. The third thing was a pair of nylons.

Kayo had no need for nylons. Since the war had ended, she wore pants, rolled up at the ankles, too large, but right for her now that she worked long, hard hours scrubbing clothes. Even if she wore skirts, she would never wear nylons. She was only thirteen years old.

She would give them to Isao as well. He was a natural salesman. Surely, one of these Hakodate women would want something like this at a good price. With a little effort, even a troubling gift like Quill's nylons could find some use.

Kayo stacked the last sheet into the basket. She tucked the chocolate, the nylons and the rice around the sheets and followed Quill down the hallway, past the commander's office and toward the exit. The office door was closed, and she heard language gobbledygook on the other side.

That meant she would have to wait outside before she could return to the laundry, to collect the money for the order she had delivered today. She went outside and sat on the concrete steps and placed the basket on the ground. These Americans never took off their shoes, and she didn't in the barracks either. Wearing shoes inside just wasn't natural.

"Kayo!" Isao ran toward her. He was dressed in a dirty pair of black shorts. His knees were covered with smut from the streets, his white tennis shoes were gray, and his stomach gaped through a hole in his striped shirt. Maybe she should ask Quill for a needle and thread. If he was going to leave her gifts, they might as well be useful gifts.

Kayo tried out the stern look that her mother would have given Isao under the circumstances, but she couldn't sustain it. Thinking of her mother made her think about crying. She knew she was failing Isao when she didn't scold him for skipping school. "What are you doing here?"

"Working," he said. "Like you. Did the *gaijin* give you anything today?"

Kayo produced the nylons and the chocolate. "See what you can do with these."

Isao let the nylons dangle from his hand. They floated in the air like *bonito* flakes. "Hunh," said Isao. "These don't seem very sturdy."

"It doesn't matter. Women will want them. You should take them to the Comfort Center, see if any women want them there."

Isao shook his head. "They closed it, remember?"

Kayo's lips thinned. "Yes. Now I remember. Well, someone will want them."

"Maybe you should keep them and see if anyone at the laundry wants them. Maybe old Mrs. Sasa wants to look sexy. Or she wants to give them to one of her girls."

She cuffed Isao, and he winced. "That is for disrespecting your elders," said Kayo. "If Mrs. Sasa didn't give me work, you and I would starve." Kayo thought. "Should I give them to her as a thank you present?"

"No!" Isao shoved the delicate nylons into his pocket. "We live in the new Japan. It's all about money and democracy.

There are no more gifts without motive. You need to be more ruthless. Like a fox. Like an American."

"But Mrs. Sasa—"

Isao's voice lowered. "She would fire you on the spot if she knew we were *hibakusha*. They believe that we are freaks because of the bomb. Don't paint her as our savior. She uses young girls to make a killing off GI Joe's laundry. Don't let her talk you into doing anything else."

Kayo wanted to scold Isao, to remind him of who was the oldest, but he had learned so much. He could speak English. He could make money out of dust. She said nothing.

The door to the barracks opened. Kayo dusted off her baggy pants. As she stood, one long, skinny braid whipped over her shoulder. The American commander had an envelope for her, written in English letters. "*Kane*," he said, massacring the Japanese word for money. It didn't matter. She took the envelope.

Out the door behind him came a strange man. She'd never seen his like. Her first thought was *akuma*, a demon. This man was black, with hair that clung to his skull in black and grey whorls. He dressed like an American army officer, the same army uniform, but different patches than the rest of them. Not taking her eyes off him, Kayo stumbled down the steps next to her basket. She gathered Isao to her side. Isao's mouth gaped open.

The man towered over the commander, a full head taller. "Hey Isao," said the commander. "Glad you're here. Dr. Marsh needs someone to help him, and I thought about you."

"They're talking about you," said Kayo. "What are they saying?"

"They want me to help that man. He is a doctor."

The *akuma* man knelt so he could look Isao in the eye. Kayo looked away, as direct eye contact was rude. She was ashamed that Isao met the man's gaze without flinching. "Hello," *akuma* man said in accented Japanese.

"Hey Joe," said Isao in English. He went on into a strange patter that Kayo recognized as his merchant talk.

"No," said *akuma* man in better Japanese than Kayo expected. "I don't want to buy anything from you. I need a guide. I hear you know what I'm looking for."

"What are you looking for, Marsh-*sensei*?" Isao couldn't pronounce the "r" and the word was Ma-shu. English had some stupid sounds.

"I'm a biologist. I focus on the effects of radiation."

Kayo's stomach tightened. Were they looking to study people? There were already scientists in Nagasaki and back in Hiroshima, studying people with their hair falling out and their skin sagging off their faces, burns and sickness and death. So far, Kayo and Isao had not been sick, but every day she lived in fear of it. She did not want to be alone in the world. She didn't want to die.

Isao shook his head. His smile sparkled. "Marsh-*sensei*, you are in the wrong city."

"I've heard there's something outside of town. You could help me look."

Kayo shook her head. She had heard about it too. They talked about it at the laundry. Some sort of mutated animal, a fantasy, they said. But she didn't think so. She thought that when the Americans came with their poisonous bomb, that Japan's guardians would not let this pass, and now they were awake. Maybe that was also her fantasy, one that kept her moving forward.

Isao had that gleam in his eye, the one that sealed a deal. "You want me to guide you?"

"Yes. I need someone who knows the area to help me."

"I am afraid," said Kayo, studying her feet, "that my brother and I are new here. Perhaps another boy would be better."

Isao pulled himself up, and pointed at himself, middle finger to nose. "I'm your guide," he said. "We may be new here, but I've been everywhere."

Kayo winced inside. Did he ever go to school at all? She hoped her parents would forgive her.

"That's what they tell me," said Marsh. "Then tomorrow we'll get started."

<hr>

Kayo's hands were becoming red and scaly from the harsh soap of the laundry. She wrapped strips of cloth around them when they weren't in the water. She and Isao sat in the tiny room they occupied, eating dinner by a dim lantern. Isao took the small bowl of rice from her and dug in, chopsticks flashing like blades.

"Not so fast," said Kayo. "That's all you get tonight."

"Soon," said Isao, "we'll have more. I'll take that American everywhere. Except where he could find anything." He picked a grain of rice off his upper lip and popped it in his mouth.

"There's nothing to find," said Kayo. "Don't you feel ashamed, taking advantage of that man?"

"No," said Isao. He uncrossed his legs and poured her a small cup of hot water. They could not afford tea. "We must take advantage of them. Besides, there is something out there. He doesn't need to find it right away, that's all."

"One of the guardians?" Kayo smiled. She sipped the water. The Americans had brought clean water, and tea or not, it was a blessing to have it.

Isao nodded. "Not the *kirin*, the dragon, or the phoenix. They all flew away when the bomb came. But the turtle. Now, the turtle is slow. The turtle wants vengeance for Japan."

Isao would pick the turtle. He loved them and had kept several over the years. "For our family," said Kayo.

"For our army," said Isao.

"If you found the turtle," said Kayo, "I would not be displeased."

———•••———

Her *kami* eyes failed her when Quill touched her shoulder. She sprang away from him, putting a bed between him and her. "It's okay," said Quill. That much English she understood. His freckles made him look like a spotted salamander and his red hair repulsed her. He spewed out some English and started toward her.

She slipped past him and ran into the hall, past the commander and Marsh. The commander asked her something in a concerned voice, but she didn't stop running until she was outside. She ran to the laundry without the basket, without the sheets and without the payment for the last load, her throat coated with the metallic taste of fear.

The laundry was a swampy quagmire of humidity, like a hot Hiroshima day in the summer. Old women stirred a giant vat of clothes, scrubbed clothes on washboards, and toted baskets of clothes to drying racks. Coming down the stairs from Mrs. Sasa's office, two young women wearing Western dresses blew kisses at their boss. Mrs. Sasa walked from station to station, supervising the work of her employees. She noted Kayo's appearance.

"What is it, Kayo-*chan*?" She placed a solicitous hand on Kayo's shoulder, her nails like the talons of a dragon.

Kayo shook her head. She had no idea what to say.

"Where's the money for the order?"

"I forgot it."

Mrs. Sasa puckered her lips. "That's not like you."

"I'm sorry," she said.

"You come into my office," said Mrs. Sasa.

The noise of the laundry diminished a little as Mrs. Sasa slid her door shut. She tapped her finger on her chin. "What is this about?"

"Nothing," said Kayo. "I saw a mouse in the barracks. I was afraid."

Mrs. Sasa laughed. "There isn't a woman in Japan afraid of a mouse anymore. Try again, little liar."

Kayo shifted and listened to the floorboards creak.

"Was one of the GIs mean to you?"

Tears rimmed in Kayo's eyes. "No. Not mean."

Mrs. Sasa could afford tea. She poured Kayo a cup, sat at a low table, and patted the *tatami* beside her. "Kayo," she said, "I don't know what happened, but I think I can guess. How old are you?"

"Thirteen."

"And you are not a woman?"

"No. Not yet."

"I feel sorry for you. I know you have no mother. You mustn't feel ashamed of a man being attracted to you. You must take advantage of it."

"I can't."

"A soldier gives you gifts. Isao told me when he tried to sell me nylons last week. You accept these gifts."

Kayo nodded.

"You must," said Mrs. Sasa. "It is a very practical thing to do in your situation, but you must know that any American wants something in return for their investment. They aren't like us. Give this man what he wants. There will be more gifts, better gifts."

"I can't do that," whispered Kayo. "I can't."

Mrs. Sasa's hand covered the top of Kayo's. "I am only giving you advice. It is such a little thing to give for such a good return. After the first time, you will feel no fear." She laughed. "You will only be bored. Get pretty things for yourself, get food for your brother."

"I can't."

Mrs. Sasa shrugged. "I can only give you my opinion. What you do is up to you. Now, I need you to go back to the barracks and get my money."

"Can someone else go?"

"No," said Mrs. Sasa. "That will remain your job."

———

The eyes of Private Quill followed her whenever he thought there were no officers looking. Kayo avoided his eyes and didn't go into any room with him unless someone else was there. Quill stopped leaving her gifts. That was fine as long as Isao led Marsh around the countryside, but the money that Isao made from cigarettes, chocolates and the other knickknacks was essential. They could never afford rice without Quill.

One night Isao bought home fish. Kayo scolded him. "We need to save our money."

"We need fish," said Isao. "Just this once."

"No," said Kayo. "Quill doesn't give me gifts to sell anymore."

"Well, Marsh-*sensei* keeps giving me money." Isao lifted bits of fish to his mouth. "I like him. He's been teaching me about genetic mutation."

"What's that?"

"Sometimes when you are irradiated, it can change you."

Kayo had bad dreams about that. "It has not changed you or me."

"You," said Isao.

"What do you mean?"

"I mean that I've mutated into a rich man."

"So, he thinks that this creature you're looking for is a mutation? Not a turtle?"

Isao shrugged. "If an animal mutates, it could become anything. You know, a dog, or a *tanuki* could have two heads or something." Isao puffed as he chewed the hot fish. "With Marsh-*sensei* in my pocket, we don't need Quill. Besides, I think I could convince the *sensei* to take us to America."

Kayo clucked in disgust. "Marsh-*sensei* will leave. There is no mutated monster, and he will make science somewhere else." She chewed on her lower lip. "We need Quill."

"Why did he stop giving you gifts?" said Isao. "Did you make him mad?"

"In a way," said Kayo. She made up her mind. She pushed her fish away.

"Don't you want it?"

"No. You can have mine. Come with me tomorrow. I need you to translate some English for me."

<hr>

Kayo brushed her hair and left it out, black, smooth and glossy. She borrowed a dress from one of Mrs. Sasa's girls, belted at the waist to hide how baggy it was on her. Mrs. Sasa offered some lipstick, suggesting that it would make her look more adult, but Kayo didn't want to look more adult. Part of her hoped that if she looked thirteen, Quill would go back to the way things were before.

He didn't though. When she entered the barracks with her laundry basket and Isao, he watched her as though she were laid on a small ceramic plate with *wasabi* and ginger, especially for his eyes. When she explained to Isao what she thought Quill wanted and what she needed his English for, they had argued. In the end Isao had agreed to speak for her, but he was angry and ashamed.

Isao's narrow eyes were like a microscope, boring into Quill. "My sister says that she doesn't mind if you date her. As long as you give us a full bag of rice and enough money to buy good food each month."

Quill pinched Kayo's hair between thumb and forefinger and rattled off something to Isao. "He says that he'll do that." Isao gestured with his hands as he and Quill negotiated. Kayo knew they were talking about the exact amount of yen that Kayo would be worth a month.

Then it was done. For a bag of rice and money for fruit and fish, she was a prostitute to an American. They wouldn't go hungry. She was nauseous.

"He says tomorrow night. Come here. I know a place in the country he can take you."

Quill disappeared and returned with two envelopes, one for the laundry, one with some yen for her. He outlined her jaw with a finger, kissed her on the forehead and they left. Outside, she hugged herself with her hands to stop shaking.

Isao plucked the envelope away from her. He counted the money. "This is more than we've seen in a month, Kayo. More than Marsh-*sensei* gives me." He put it in the dirty pocket of his shorts.

"Give it to me," said Kayo. "I need to buy our dinner."

"No," said Isao. His face was hard. "I keep the money."

She raised her hand to slap him, but she put it down again, and she didn't look at him. Her tears splattered in the dirt, her fists clenched at her sides. Kayo's tears blinded her as she made her way back to the laundry.

Before meeting Quill, Kayo let Mrs. Sasa use rouge and lipstick to paint her face. Mrs. Sasa began to talk about how Kayo might like to date other men, to make more money. She could arrange things and keep a small fee. Kayo said no. It was bad enough that there was the fact of Quill. She would not sink that low. Mrs. Sasa helped Kayo pile her hair upon her head, like a Hollywood starlet. Kayo felt very unlike herself, which made her feel better about everything. She thought about the woman she looked like on the outside. This woman was not Kayo. She was someone else.

At the barracks, she navigated the stairs unbalanced, teetering in borrowed pumps. Quill leaned on a counter, scowling. He said something in English and pointed at his watch. Kayo knew she was late. He grabbed her wrist. Tonight he looked like a hungry tiger, and she knew that while she would walk through her life for the rest of her years, tonight Quill would eat the piece of her that was alive.

They drove an American jeep out to a farm in the country, an old-fashioned house with torn paper jagged in the *shoji* doors. She and Isao had stayed here on their way from Hiroshima to Hakodate. No one was here now, the house too far from town, too old to be of use to the Americans.

Quill spat out a wad of gum. He had also gone to some effort to look nice, his hair slicked back, and his uniform brushed and straightened, like he was some Joe taking his girl to the movies. He reached for her across the seat and pulled her in from the small of her back, and he kissed her. His tongue pushed into her mouth like a snake, a swollen thing that made her gag. She squirmed to get away. He clenched her to his body. She froze like a rabbit, only her mind active, screaming the word no over and over.

He stopped and said something in English, sharp and mean. There was only hunger in his eyes. He had paid. They had a deal. With shame, she began unbuttoning the top three buttons of her dress, her fingers clumsy, her hands trembling. She thought about what she needed to do to make sure that she and Isao survived. Rice. Water. Fish.

Quill placed a hand down her bra, over a tiny budding breast. She winced and closed her eyes. His fingers played with the hooks, and he leaned her back on the car seat. She riveted her eyes shut. He was everywhere.

Then abruptly Quill disappeared.

Kayo opened her eyes. Marsh dangled Quill by the collar of his shirt, his fist cocked back, ready to strike Quill like a temple bell. The *akuma* man stood a foot over Quill, dangerous. No, not a demon. An avenging bodhisattva.

Behind them, Isao rocked on his feet, a satisfied cat, sunning itself in the light of success. He opened the jeep door and helped her out. "Run, Kayo. Not toward the house."

The ground shook with the tremor of an earthquake. Kayo jumped out of the rocking car and onto the side of her ankle, just as she had feared because of the pumps. She abandoned the shoes. The ground shook again, jarring. Over the tree line, part of mountain moved, a hill of green.

"See," Isao yelled over the roar that filled the night like an air raid siren. "Good value for the money, *sensei*." Isao stared at the creature, and it turned in their direction. Kayo knew then. He was controlling the monster. At least she thought he might be. Both of them what Marsh called mutations.

Marsh dropped Quill, who jabbered some frantic English and raced toward the house. A dome, a giant, green-shelled turtle, blended into the pines of the mountain so that when it slept, the people of Hakodate would not see it.

Now the turtle was awake. Isao stared at it, standing his ground. "You are the protector of children!" he yelled. "That man is yours!"

Marsh grabbed Kayo's arm and they swerved out of the monster's path. The turtle lumbered on stalky pillars. Its tail leveled trees, and its shell plowed the ground as it plodded toward Quill.

Quill beelined for the dilapidated house. He scrambled into the crawl space. She imagined his screams drowned out by the air raid siren of the *kaiju's* shrieking roar.

Kayo heard Isao shout, or it might have been in her head. "Protect my sister. Protect Japan."

The turtle stamped the house in its path flat. It exploded into splinters, frames, mats and rot. Kayo couldn't look at another explosion, more destruction. Crumbling and crunching crescendoed and died. The night became silent. The turtle turned back to Isao, who touched its beak as it bent down. Then it plodded back to the mountains, back to its sleep.

Isao pulled Quill's money out of his pocket, dropped it, and ground the white envelope into the grass with his dirty tennis shoe. "We will never spend a penny of that money," he said. "You will tell Mrs. Sasa you are not interested in any more of her ideas, and you will quit the laundry."

Kayo shook her head. "How will we live? I must do something. I must take care of you."

Isao took her hand. "We've managed before. We'll do so now."

Kayo kissed his forehead, and he wiped glossy red lipstick off with the back of his hand.

Marsh spoke in Japanese. "Kayo, are you okay?"

Kayo clutched her dress across her chest and bowed. "Thank you very much, *sensei.*"

"Don't worry about it. Isao told me tonight we'd find a monster. We did, but we got here in time." He crossed his arms and studied Isao. "You've been holding out on me."

Isao put his hands up in the air and smiled at Marsh. "No, I haven't. I promised you we'd find your mutation. What will the commander say when you tell him Quill is dead?"

"That Quill wasn't the only monster here." Marsh ran a hand over his head. "I mean, that was an accident. That would never happen again, right?"

"No," said Isao. "Never."

The turtle once again tucked into the mountains. Kayo watched the pines shift on the mountains behind it and felt Isao's eyes watching her, and the sleepy eyes of the turtle. She felt protected. She felt safe.

This story has been around a little bit. First it appeared in Paper Golem's Cucurbital 3. *Then it found a home in the anthology* Abandoned Places. *And now, finally, I've put it in a collection of my own.*

I read the story of Susy Clemen's death and thought it was one of the most tragic and lonely endings I had ever heard about. More research showed me a complicated and troubled relationship with her parents, especially her father. This story is the result of my musings in that regard. The ending of the story makes me surprisingly hopeful.

Mark Twain's Daughter

Every time Susy stayed in the Hartford house, she told herself there was no need to fear the dark. Alone, she rattled around the house, a pebble in a boot. The house was going to swallow her, but she was afraid to leave it.

Temperature had canceled her trip to Europe with her family. When they lived in Europe, Susy shined. She worried that her parents had discarded her. Jealousy of her sister Clara, who was traveling with them, glowed like a coal inside of her. Clara could do no wrong and Susy could do no right. Susy, who had loved a married man. And a woman. No wonder her parents hadn't protested when she stayed in the States.

Of course, she would be missed, and Susy wondered if her father left her behind because he was jealous of her. Her stories, his friends said, were like Mark Twain's, smart and brilliant. And her voice. Madame Marchesi confided in her that she was her greatest student. Mark Twain never wanted anyone in his family to get more attention than him.

Susy's fingers trailed in the dust that coated the grand banister, just like the powder Madame Marchesi patted on Susy's shoulders before she sang at a recital. Dust motes carouseled like European waltzers.

When the fever had started, Katy, the family friend who looked after her, cajoled Susy to come home with her. Still stinging with anger about her abandonment, Susy stayed alone. She hadn't counted on resentment turning to regret.

Dusk bleached away the last of the reception hall colors. The covered furniture glowed albino in the cavernous entry. Susy massaged similes and metaphors as she descended the stairs. Like her father, always playing with words. The covered furniture. Sails? Souls? Seraphim wings? Sea foam?

Sea foam. The tumultuous waves of her family's gifts churned at Hartford. Clara's piano concertos, Father's ink-stained manuscripts, her own scribblings choked the air and the memory. Clemens' art decayed inside the walls.

The house tilted around her. Susy grasped the banister for balance. She would sink like a stone under the surface of the house.

When she steadied herself again, Count de Calry studied her from the bottom step, white gloves in one hand, shiny top hat in the other. He expected an invisible servant to take his accessories away, but there was only Susy.

She panicked. Where had he come from? Her parents would never allow his visit. Her grin was lopsided. Her parents weren't here. If they had decided she was unacceptable, unacceptable she would be.

In the deserted kitchen, there were no tea or dainties to offer. He had caught her in her nightgown, cheeks flushed. Then again, Susy was certain the count had seen his wife in *deshabille* before.

Mama loved Count de Calry as much as Susy did, even though both their loves were wicked love. Susy lifted her nightdress ever so slightly, cautious not to show too much ankle. She descended slowly, elegantly, deportment lessons guiding her. Straighten your spine. Throw your shoulders back. Glide lightly and slowly. Keep your neck long.

The brilliant gleam of the count's white teeth winked in the dimming hall. On the bottom step, Susy extended her arm. Her hand stopped with a flourish beyond the lace of her sleeve, waiting for the count to touch it with his lips, the charming habit of the European gentleman.

Instead, the count spread his arms, inviting her to his embrace.

Suzy became a sculpture. What would the embrace of the count be like? He could never guess all the nights she imagined this very thing, this sweet and forbidden invitation. It was a delicious fear. Would his arms feel the same as Louise's?

She inched forward, a tiny step. Her fingers brushed his coat. Her heart fluttered. All was the metallic smell of radiating heat. No matter. She knew the smell of his cologne well enough to conjure it.

Red light flashed across her vision as the count sizzled away. Susy stepped away from the apparition. She clutched at the banister. Her mother said Susy was delicate. Her father said she was artistic. Maybe what society whispered about her was true. Maybe Susy Clemens had little grasp of reality.

Susy's head throbbed as she stumbled back up the steps. Hot tears streamed down her arid skin. Where had he gone?

On the second floor landing she wrapped her arms around her knees and lay on her side, tucking her feet under her nightgown. She wanted her father to soothe her, to put a cool cloth on her head, to tell her a story. Resting on the polished wood, her body circled protectively around her empty heart.

———•••———

Susy was so parched that the flesh in the back of her throat clicked when she swallowed. She pushed herself away from the floor. The wood where she had lain heated her fingers. She leaned against the wallpaper and fought her way down the hall. Shadows reached for her and the ground lurched upwards. When she reached the doorway of her room, she stumbled toward her bed and landed where she collapsed. Her breath wheezed. Her nightgown smothered her chest. She wanted to claw it off.

Water rimmed the bottom third of the glass on her night-stand. Two swallows, maybe. Her hand shook as she reached for it, and she backhanded the glass onto the floor. It shattered like a diamond rain.

Susy sat up. Leaning sideways, her forehead touched the cool metal of her bed's frame. She dangled her feet over the side of the bed and stared at the table and pitcher, miles across the room. The tiny puddle on the floor spread like a swift current, a river raging between her and the opposite wall.

Susy used the inside of her wrist to wipe the sweat out of her eyes. There was no choice. She resolved to swim to the other side of the room, but as soon as she put her toe in the current, it felt too rapid. Her right eye twitched. The bed be-came a dock and the splinters of it needled her through her nightgown. When Katy came in the morning, she would find her dead of thirst.

"I'll get water for you," the Prince of Wales said.

Edward turned up the gaslight. The flame flickered like tongues of sequins. Her eyes focused on a mirror image. She and Edward had the same brown hair and eyes. She had acted Edward, son of King Henry the Eighth, and Clara had played Tom Canty from Mark Twain's book. Mama and Papa had been delighted with Susy's performance. Back when Papa still loved her.

Edward walked across the surface of the river and sat down beside her on the uncomfortable wooden mattress, dressed in his velvets, his eyes, her eyes, so wide and clear. What Susy wanted to say was that the future King of England must not serve her, but her throat creaked.

Edward held a glass of water to Susy's lips. She gulped the water, hoping it would drown the heat.

"Your majesty," she said, her voice rasping.

"You and I," Edward said, with gentle consideration. "We have traded places before."

"We did," Susy said. "When I was young."

"It is only right that I take care of you, after you have granted me such a boon."

Susy ran her fingers through her tangled hair. "You could trade places with me again," Susy said. "Would you like to be Mark Twain's daughter?"

Edward's face was blank. "When we were young, I could pretend to be a girl, if I had to, but never a grown woman. Now it is impossible."

The light hurt Susy's eyes. "It is no trial," Susy said. "I pretend to be a grown woman all the time."

"Are you thirsty?" Edward asked, offering the glass again. She hadn't seen him refill it.

"No," Susy said. She splashed her feet in the river on the floor and felt the stickiness of blood as she cut herself on shards of glass.

"I can understand why you want to run away," said Edward.

"Your life is no different," said Susy. "You have to pretend to be a king. That must be much harder than pretending to be a woman."

"I will die young," said Edward. "Therefore, I will avoid the whole affair. What do you say to that solution?"

Susy reclined back on the hard bed. "I agree. Better to get it all over with at once, rather than dying incrementally." The light faded. Edward's gentle hand stroked her matted hair and she drifted into fitful sleep.

Restlessness drove Susy downstairs. Her feet hurt like the mermaid with new legs, each step like stabbing knives. She could not lower her chin to her chest because the movement stabbed her neck. There were no counts with feral teeth in the bright morning sun. She shielded her eyes, not looking at the window.

Her face was bloated with fever. It radiated out from her as if she were the sun. Silhouetted by light was a boy. Edward? Her eyes blinked tears. As the boy drew the draperies closed, he transformed into a girl, her hair chopped like the prince's, her eyes staring beyond Susy at God. Joan of Arc, her father's obsession.

Joan's eyes were the same as Susy's, as Edward's. They all looked through the same eyes and saw the same things. She was dressed in Christ's armor, gleaming, cool.

Susy twirled a finger in the nest of her hair. "I am sick."

"I can see that," Joan said.

Susy stood as straight as possible. Raise the head. Elongate the neck. "I have no desire to see you," Susy said. She hated Joan. "You will want to see my father."

"I have come on his account since he is unable to come himself."

Hysteria fluttered in Susy's chest. The center of her father's universe was moving far away from her. He would never forgive her for being talented. "I thought he couldn't bear to be apart from you."

Joan's voice held the condescension she would not allow her serene countenance to show. "Yet, he asked me to come, and so I did. You know how he feels about you."

Too well, Susy thought. "I am a disappointment to my father in all things," Susy said, studying a spot of embossed trim over Joan's head. "That is why he made you."

"What you say is *verite*." Joan shrugged. Even though the room was dim, the armor found light to reflect. "Yet he pities your weakness, and he wants me to comfort you."

Susy sank to the lower steps and buried her head in her hands.

"I only mean to tell you the truth," said Joan. She sat by Susy. "God wants us to be truthful. I do not mean that your father does not love you."

"You are so certain of yourself," said Susy. "That's what drew him to you."

"You are his angel. He loves your caprice and your voice. You do not know you are an angel because you do not allow yourself to fly. That is why he likes me better. Because He made me with purpose."

"Father or God?"

Joan helped Susy to stand, and they crossed the room to the draped window. "He loves you just the same. That should give you something to live for."

Susy blinked at the small seam of light that showed her Hartford outside. In the distance, traffic flowed like any other day, people walking, riding in carriages, sprinting to the trolley cars. "There's nothing for me out there," she said. "I would much rather stay in here."

"You must not think that way," said Joan, her eyebrow arching with disapproval. "He has a purpose for everyone."

Again, Susy wondered if Joan meant her father or God. She wanted to yell at Joan, but her voice came out pathetic and weak. "How can you say that?"

"You continue to deny your gifts," said Joan. "If you listen, you can do anything."

"Oh yes," Susy said. Even with her voice barely audible, she could hear the peevish tones she hated creep into it. "The world is mine. Up go the trolley cars for Mark Twain's daughter. Down go the trolley cars for Mark Twain's daughter."

"Pray to God" said Joan. "Pray for comfort."

"I can't be what Papa wants." Susy whispered. "I can only be myself."

"Then it is inevitable. Death will take you." Joan faded into the gloom, boots echoing in the dining hall.

As evening fell, Katy found Susy sitting on the floor, tracing wings in the dust.

"Oh darling," said Katy. "Let me help you back to bed.

Susy's glassy eyes looked at Katy. "Why did Papa cut my wings?"

—◆◆◆—

Susy awoke, wailing with the certainty her mother had died. She covered her face with her hands. Her shoulders convulsed and her body shook. She had to find her mother.

Katy had cleaned up the glass, and the riverbed was dry now. Susy groped her way across the floor. In the closet, she saw her mother hanging from the bar, eyes grotesque, tongue bulging.

Susy staggered to her feet, her eyes darting wildly. She hated Clara. How dare Clara not take care of Mama! How dare she allow Mama to despair and hang herself! Clara wrote Susy about the courts of India, about the nature of New Zealand, happy in her good fortune, and their mother hung dead in Hartford.

Susy grasped the silkiness of her mother's dress. Her sobs cascaded down her body. "Poor Mama! Poor, poor Mama! Let me close your eyes, Mama!"

Her mother's body dangled like a bell pull. There was no weight to the body, no flesh, only bone, like her skeleton and clothes were all that were left. Susy stared at the desiccated skull and empty eyes. "Poor sweet Mama!" Her shoulders ached as she reached up. "Let me close your eyes!"

Katy cracked the door to the closet. Light made Susy shield her eyes. She plucked at her mother's hem. "Oh, Katy! Mama is gone!"

Katy's thick arms circled her shoulders. "Your mama is fine, Susy!"

"Look at her...her..." The words died in Susy's mouth. She clutched the dress, felt her mother's bones crunch against her chest.

"Sweetheart," said Katy, "that's not your mama. That is your housecoat." Katy helped her to her feet. "Let me help you back to bed."

Susy clutched the robe to her, holding her mother tight. She would never let her go.

———◆◆———

The moonlight did not hurt Susy's eyes. She stood in front of the window. Her feet were bound like a Chinese lady's and her hair was wild like a Chinese demon's. Her nightgown puddled on the floor.

Katy said she would return with the doctor. Her goodbye kiss sizzled on Susy's forehead.

Heat made her restless. On the landing, Susy's body was pure and miraculous.

Joan muttered prayers behind her. Soon they would take Joan to the stake. They did not believe Joan talked to God. Susy didn't either.

"The last hours are the cruelest," said Joan. She rose from kneeling and crossed herself, gazing into Heaven.

"Knowing what your death will be," Susy said.

"I will never die," said Joan. "God will take me to him, and I will live by his side regardless of what they do to me."

"You will never die," Susy agreed. "Papa would never stand for it."

Joan directed her gaze away from Heaven, her face lit with the divine. Susy knelt and pulled her nightgown over her shoulders. She shuddered. Strange and naked in the moonlight, she was too vulnerable to be seen by an agent of God.

"You will die," pronounced Joan. "Mark Twain's daughter."

Joan's beatific glow hurt Susy's eyes. Susy twisted her hair over her right shoulder. "Why?"

"He is replacing you with me. I am the final version," said Joan. "You are no longer needed. It pains me to tell you the truth. Yet, as I am, I cannot lie to you."

Susy squinted to see her. "I think it doesn't pain you in the least. Susy no longer needs to exist where there is Joan. That's what you mean."

"He wrote you wrong," said Joan. "You're not what he intended at all. You are too artistic and ephemeral. It is hard for a character without a center to carry a story."

Susy was not ashamed of the sneer in her voice. "The church could only murder you. I wonder how you will fare at Papa's hands?"

<hr>

Susy opened her eyes. Edward stood over her, hand extended.

"I did not know that you were me," she said.

"It is no matter," said Edward. "Let me take you away from Hartford. Let us leave him and go somewhere better. Let us be the center of our own world."

Susy peeled her spirit away from her body. Her flesh was wax. Her hair a cloud of brown. The rash and black fingers were hidden under white lacy sleeves. Fever flushed her cheeks with pink petals. Her corpse was pretty in a way it had not been in life, a delicate painted doll.

She grasped Edward's hand and rose up. Wings protected her chest. She unfolded them and her heart broke free. Singing with a voice that Madame Marchesi could never have imagined, she broke the surface of the past and glided into memory.

Before you read this story, I have to make sure you understand the content. This is a very triggering story. This piece is partly biographical. My family was grossly abusive. There's sexual abuse and incest herein. You might skip this story.

This story was published in Daydream Dandelions anthology Mosaics 2: A Collection of Independent Women. This story was vastly improved, thanks to the editing of Jessica West, and is easily the most painful thing I've ever written.

I know. That really makes you want to read it. If you choose to, be prepared for misery.

Cookies

Really? Okay. Honestly, I've always wanted to be a psychiatrist's soundtrack, so knock yourself out. I don't know what to tell you. If you'd talked to me before the fire, I was pretty sure I had it all figured out. My life, I mean. I had that all figured out. That was before my brother Egghead told me my brother Jack was homeless.

No, Egghead isn't really his name. His name is Jason. Egghead is what Jack and I have called him since he was a baby and he had no hair. No, he's not super smart.

Okay, so you need to know about my family. Our mother is a clinger. She built a web made out of the stickiest guilt and we children fought hard to untangle from it. I was born with a good knife, and I slashed my way out, but the strands of the web keep pulling me back when I should most stay away, because I'm pulled in by the urge to fix everything. Which is how my childhood was spent. Fixing everything.

I call my mother, with absolutely no affection, the Spider.

Yes, write that down. While you're at it, underline it three times in that little notebook of yours. Do that.

There's three of us and the Spider. There was my dad, Frank, but he's gone now, in a dead guy kind of way. My younger brother Jason, AKA Egghead, right? He's had a job for almost a year, an all-time record for him, and he's living in low rent housing with the Spider, taking care of her now that her health is really bad instead of pretend bad. You know, aging, as opposed to undiagnosed depression and faking episodes of illness when your kids aren't obedient enough. The Spider is a great believer in Munchausen's Syndrome and its uses. Egghead needs to live with the Spider, otherwise he'd be homeless. In spite of our past, Egghead and the Spider get along well. He blames the Spider for nothing. He blames Jack, who screwed him for most of his childhood and adolescence. Yes, I do mean the physical act.

My episode, note my finger quotes, is all about Jack. Jack was beaten by our mother, fucked by our father, and found ways to creatively express his anger and fear by taking it out on his younger siblings: beating me and fucking Jason. Mind, I see my whole family as a seething, festering pool of cess, bubbling and belching filth into the air. Typical small-town family. Good times. Jack lived with the Spider until recently, sort of a mutually dysfunctional agreement.

One day, Egghead popped by my house. Edgar, my husband, and I live in a typical ranch in a nice neighborhood. Egghead has a rusted-out minivan, so I'm sure the neighbors thought I was doing a meth deal.

That was meant to be funny.

Anyway, Egghead sat at my kitchen table when he told me, drinking a bottle of Coke, his dirty fingernails wet with bottle sweat. "Honest to God," he said to me, "her face shattered when Jack hit her. It sounded like the car that rear-ended me last year." *Crunch. Crack.*

Yeah, that bumper was still broken, right outside in the drive-way. "That's it then. She's finally going to do it."

"I think so."

"You know what happened the last time." And the last time. And the time before that.

"This time she'll do it. She needs plastic surgery."

I nodded and sipped water. The last three times, before I had broken it off with everyone but Egghead, she and Egghead had taken a restraining order all the way to court. She backed out every time. The first time I called her.

"How could you do that to Jason?" I yelled at her. Whenever I talked to the Spider, I forgot to use my indoor voice.

She sighed like the martyr she wanted to be. "Jack has no place to go. You know I would do anything for you kids."

As upset as Egghead was those three times, he couldn't bring himself to cut the Spider off. When you're used to watching a train wreck all your life, your eyes stay on the track.

Besides, the official family scapegoat was Jack.

You know the term scapegoat, right? I read it in a psychology text, so I figure you ran across it in school, right?

Moving on. Over the course of time, I avoided all the family stuff. For Chrissakes, I am the smart one. I went to college and can fake normal on a pretty good day. I'm married, and I have a very successful job, and a successful marriage, and by God, I'm a success. I mentioned by the time the Spider got a court or-der against Jack for breaking her face, I'd already walked away. Hubs and I didn't want to keep dipping our toes into the pool of domestic violence, and you know, tough love and protect yourself, so we avoided them all. Then you still feel like shit, we all do, but there it is. Save yourself.

Jack is technically what they call a bad guy. He was married for about a minute and he beat his wife. No, I don't know the details. I don't even know her. Jack's violent, he's a bully, and he wants to call all the shots. I was hoping for jail for him, because that'd be a good place for him to end up. Three squares, warmth, a nice, controlled environment.

I liked him when we were little, before Frank and the Spider started abusing us. Jack and I were tiny kids on the beach, making a sandcastle, Egghead not too far away on a blanket. I've been thinking a lot about the girl I was since you and I started talking. I think about Jack too.

When we were really little, Jack and I would play house. I wanted him to be the dad, but he had different ideas.

"I want to be Mommy," he said. He wrapped the floral apron I borrowed from the kitchen drawer around his waist.

"No!" I stamped my foot on the floor. "That's not how it works. You can't be Mommy! Only girls can be Mommy!"

"I'm the mommy."

He pretended to cook, and I wrapped a tie around my neck and came home from work.

The difference between Jack and me? I made choices not to become like our parents. The thing about Jack is that he's a coward. You want to know how I know?

Jack is concerned about one thing: saving his own skin. The question isn't why wouldn't he. The question is why aren't Egghead and I as messed up as Jack? Egghead is pretty messed up, but not in Jack's league. Like I said, I can fake a good normal.

There was this time when I was nine that Jack had scarfed the last of the cookies the Spider had made, and, woah, was the Spider mad.

You never knew when Spider would go off. We got home from school, and we were all hungry, starving by seven o'clock.

Any other day, she wouldn't have cared about the cookies. That day, she and Frank had a fight, I think. I don't remember about what. He went to his night shift at the gas station, and we came home from school straight into the lion's den.

The Spider snapped at us about the house being gross and about how the dining room table was piled up with dishes for five days and how we never helped around the house. She started to clear off the table to make room to make dinner, clanking pots and pans around. Then she saw the lid was off the cookie jar she had made way back when she took ceramics class, one of those few precious items to survive our bad behavior and her own tantrums. It was a teddy bear, and the head was screwed off at the neck. The headless bear was empty. God only knew where those last four cookies had gone. She went ballistic.

"Ungrateful!" was what she yelled. For all the Spider's faults, she never used bad language and still doesn't. She beat Jack with the nearest thing she could grab, a dirty wooden spoon. He howled, begging her to stop, and he raced outside, the broken screen door spanking the doorframe. Then she turned to Egghead and raised the spoon. I got in front of Egghead and backed away from her. She herded us out the door and then we heard the lock click.

We waited in winter weather with no coats. I knocked on the door, but the Spider wasn't answering. "We gotta go back in," I said. Both Egghead and I knew it was Jack. "You gotta tell her."

"I didn't do it," Jack said quietly.

I knew it was a lie. Egghead knew it was a lie. Jack was going to let us freeze.

"Tell her," I said. "We gotta go back in."

"No," said Jack. "No. It wasn't me."

I breathed in deep. The breath I let out fogged in front of me, a cone of cold, ice in my lungs and veins. I knocked on the door again. This time the Spider opened it, anger etching every age line on her face like carved ice. "What?" she spat.

"I did it," I said. "I ate the cookies."

She grabbed my hair and pulled me inside, beating me with that wooden spoon, whipping me about the legs, on my back, across my arms as they came up to protect my face. I cried but I didn't shout. That made her hit me harder.

Somewhere in the background I saw Jack and Jason come inside. Mission accomplished.

"You stand in this corner!" she yelled at me. "You don't move until I tell you to."

"I did it," said Jack. His voice shook.

The Spider sagged. "You did?" She looked at Jack.

Jack stood statue still.

"You didn't?"

"No." I cried as quietly as I could.

That was the end of the fit. We finally had bologna sandwiches and chips for supper, and I had the largest scoop of ice cream, the Spider's way of doing penance. Jack didn't get beaten. I was angry he didn't look out for us, but I didn't mind taking one for him. I knew then I could never trust him to take care of us again.

Egghead called me about a month ago. Because of the restraining order, Jack could no longer live with the Spider. Egghead moved into her apartment like some sort of nurse enforcer.

"So, where's Jack?" I said, sounding as casual as I could.

"I don't know, and I don't care."

"Does Mom know?" My mouth always has a hard time saying Mom, because I never think of the Spider as Mom.

"No." Egghead sighed. "She's worried about him."

"She would be." I rolled my eyes at Edgar, who smiled back at me. "It's kind of cold out there."

"Yeah. The homeless shelters are a joke. But like I said, I don't care."

I get that. I do. When Frank died, I wasn't happy, but part of me wanted him to die. Egghead hated Jack. It was only natural.

I didn't tell you that the Spider knew Jack was fucking Egghead, did I? She didn't do anything. She let it go on. Years later, it turns out, she knew about Frank and Jack. About Frank and me. There's got to be a special place in Hell for people like that.

When I hung up the phone, I turned to Edgar.

"I have to go. Egghead thinks Jack is homeless."

"Oh babe." Edgar wrapped me up in his arms. "What do you want to do?"

Tears came from nowhere and I was angry that I was crying. "I gotta go look for him. I don't know what I'll do. Keep him in the garage, maybe? Get him some help? I don't know."

What was I going to do? Try to help him sign up for social programs that he wouldn't follow through on? Give him some money, like a band-aid, which would do nothing to cover the gaping wounds of our childhood? Put him out of his misery like a rabid dog? At close range, I could be a pretty good shot.

Maybe try an institution.

Yeah, I see the irony in my current situation.

You might be asking yourself the big question: given all that I've told you, why on earth would I go looking for this guy? I don't have a good answer for you. Maybe the idea was that I could be Jack. There for the grace of God go I. I don't believe the grace of God line at all. Here I am still trying to fix things.

I took the day off work and loaded myself in the Elantra. Every shelter I went to, I tried to describe Jack, but I had no pictures after his high school one, so my search didn't work well. Des Moines in winter outside, underneath bridges and in boxes, is damned cold. I ate lunch at Subway and thought about the last time Jack and I really talked about anything besides the Spider.

It was at a McDonald's shortly after Frank had died. Jack and the Spider were fighting, and I had come to smooth things over.

"I think she's crazy. I think we should sign commitment papers and put her away."

Ah, the old commitment argument. Well, he was probably right. She was probably crazy. "Maybe both of you would benefit from some counseling, getting some help."

Jack rubbed a French fry in ketchup like he was stubbing out a cigarette. "You know, when I was a Navy Seal, I had my psych evaluation done. There's nothing wrong with me."

Listen, I want you to understand that Jack was never a Navy Seal. He was kicked out of the National Guard. Kicked out. I believe in his time he has been a Navy Seal, an undercover narcotics cop and a website programmer. He gives himself exciting Biker nicknames like Shadow. He lies compulsively.

I filed police reports. I visited shelters. Dead end after dead end. I left my contact information where I could, I had a good cry, sobbing about being helpless, and then I returned to my normal life.

My life. Where Egghead calls me once every four months, where I don't talk to the Spider because she endangered all of her children by staying married to Frank the rapist who died of a stroke in 1993. My life, where I live with my family of choice. It's a good life. I am damned lucky. When you come from my background, usually what you do is go out and look for the most dysfunctional partner you can find, and you relive the traditions. I'm lucky because I didn't do that.

I see what you're thinking. You're thinking I haven't dealt with all my issues.

Current evidence bears you out. I hope you aren't too smarmy about that.

One fine spring day, three months after my fruitless search, a hospital called me while I was working. "Jane Smith?"

My parents had a thing for alliteration. At least my last name wasn't Doe.

"Yes?"

"I'm calling from Metro Lutheran. Your brother is in the hospital here."

"Jason?"

"No. Jack Jenkins. He had your information, so we called you."

That hot feeling of panic spilled into my gut, acid in the back of my throat, the thing that always happened when I could feel myself getting on the train that had no brakes, the pace of my childhood life. I took a deep breath, braking, getting control, slowing down the train.

"Okay. What's wrong with him?"

I was already running through a mental list. Hit by a car. Cirrhosis. Gunshot. Pneumonia. The asshole gene had finally gone terminal.

"Burns," said the medical voice on the other end. "He's been in a fire and has some serious burns."

"Yeah, okay." The woman on the other line must have thought I was a total jerk. I had gone into that singsong voice I use when I try to pretend that everything is okay, to gloss everything over. "I'm about two hours out, but I'll be there as soon as I can be."

Then I made a quick call to Edgar, and he wanted to know if I wanted him to go with me, and I said no, not yet, let me look at the situation, and he asked if I was sure, and of course

I wasn't sure, but I lied and said, yes, I'll call you when I have more information.

On the drive there, I rehearsed what I was going to say.

"So, Jack, sorry we haven't talked in eight years. It's just that when I found your teenage Internet porn up on my computer eight Christmases ago, I thought you were a scumbag and I wanted to kill you…"

Or maybe, *"How dare you! How dare you call me! How dare you choose to be like Frank!"*

Or even, *"Jesus, stop lying. For once, just tell someone the truth, about anything."*

All of which would be really shitty things to say to someone who's homeless, has been in an accident and was horribly disfigured.

Hospitals are, well, hospitals. I'd never been to a burn ward. I checked in at the nurses' station, and they took me to Jack's room. A policeman stood outside.

If I hadn't thought of him as a stranger before, I knew he was one now. Burns covered more than seventy percent of his body, they said. His face was shriveled and raw, and the rash of flames moved up and down his arms and legs.

"We've given him something to dull the pain," the nurse said.

"This is pretty serious," I said, stating the obvious.

"Seventy-five percent of his body."

"Why the police?"

"He set the fire."

"Is he going to live?"

"We're doing what we can. You can ask the doctor more."

I sat down in the vinyl chair across from him. His skin was jagged and puddled, strange pinks and reds, pools of mottled skin. The hospital smelled like Pine-sol and plastic, but he smelled over the top of that. Once I found hot dogs in a bloated plastic bag in a park shelter by the barbecue, rancid and strangely sweet. He smelled like that.

I flipped open my cell and called home. We had a conversation, Edgar and I. He was on his way before I hung up.

Then I sat back in the chair. Jack's eyes opened and the lids were swollen and ponderous, raw. That must have hurt. He whispered.

"Hi."

I would have touched him, but that wouldn't have been wise. Emotions were complicated. Distaste, disgust, pity. A super big dose of pity, which I concentrated on. "You just rest."

"Fires," Jack said, "are the gateway to Hell."

Which of course would be right.

But that's not it at all, and that's not why we're talking.

If I had just jumped into the real story, you wouldn't understand anything at all, and you asked. "Tell me about your childhood," you said. Just like Sigmund Freud, or Thomas Dolby pretending to be Sigmund Freud. I did the next best thing. I told you about the results of my childhood.

You look puzzled. The question for you is why, right? I'm the balanced one. At least I keep saying so. How could I end up here, talking to you?

I've been thinking about that a lot, and I don't have a clear-cut answer. I didn't believe in any of that afterlife stuff anymore. I used to, as a Baptist kid, be a firm believer in Heaven and Hell, but I took one Bible study too many, and, for me, perverse human being that I am, it made me believe less in God. So, when I said that Frank should go to Hell, what I meant was that *if* there were a Hell, and *if* it was a place that punished the wicked, wouldn't *that* be the perfect place for the souls of people who raped their own children, or their brothers?

That's just too simple. There isn't a Hell any more than there is a Heaven. I like the idea that you make your Heaven here, on Earth, with the ones you love, and that Hell can also be made on Earth. In my lifetime, I've experienced both Heaven and Hell right here.

"Can I get you anything?" the policeman outside asked me.

"Don't you have to stand guard?" I asked.

"He's not going anywhere," said the policeman. "You want a cup of coffee? Anyone you want to call?"

"I called my husband."

The policeman nodded.

I fidgeted in the slick vinyl chair. "Where was he staying?" I asked.

"God's Gift. On Southeast Fourteenth. I can get you in touch with Mike Scanlon."

After, I left the hospital and hunted Mike Scanlon down. This guy, he was like an undercover religious guy. He was walking the walk, out there on the street taking care of people, not some fat cat politician pretending that being rich and Christian at the same time was simpatico with hippie Christ, who I'm down with, divine though I do not believe him to be. Mike was a Christian who wore secondhand clothes and had a scruffy three-day growth. His hand was calloused and rough when he shook mine.

"Great guy, your brother. Shame about what happened." Mike offered me a Styrofoam cup of bitter coffee that had been brewing for maybe two weeks.

I blinked. "Great guy? We are talking about Jack Jenkins, right?"

"Yeah, okay. Maybe I know a Jack Jenkins you don't. Jack was a pretty hard case when he came to us, but he was turning it around. Jack asked Jesus to save him. He cleaned himself up and served up meals. He'd talk to his old buddies during the free meals and try to get them to understand about Christ's forgiveness. Every church service he'd hand out the hymnals, and he'd started volunteering for Habitat during the day. He asked us if he could join our staff. We were thinking about it. That's the night he set the place on fire."

"Now *that's* my brother Jack. If he has a good thing going, he's got to destroy it."

"Sure. I can see why you'd think that. But it wasn't simple like that. He talked to me before he bunked down for the night. Said your dad was a sinner, like he'd been. Jack said if he could be saved, surely your dad could too. I said there was always a chance, and some interpretations of the Bible suggest salvation even after death."

I almost dropped my cup. "Forgiveness?" I laughed. "All you have to do is ask, and *poof!* all the harm you've done is washed away. No one has to make amends. No one is responsible. Thank you, Jesus."

Mike set his jaw. Damn it, if he didn't read my bitterness like a book.

"Mrs. Smith," he said. "I'm not going to tell you to forget all the harm that has been done to you and your brothers. If we follow Christ's example and we forgive, we save ourselves and others from Hell. If we don't forgive, in a way, we put ourselves and others there, and that makes us abusers."

"No." I fell into the singsong voice. "They put themselves there. And I didn't put myself in Hell, thank you very much."

"Try to think of it this way," Mike said. "You didn't deserve to be abused, and you forgave yourself for where you came from. So you're good. So did Jack, eventually. Forgiveness makes more forgiveness. With a true change of heart, people do make amends. That's why Jack, misguided, set that fire. He was trying to reach your father, I think. He thought his example might help your father find his way."

Edgar, who's more religious than me, might have said something similar. I didn't have anything to say to Mike afterwards in response. I drove around until my gas-is-empty light came on.

"Fires," Jack had said, "are the gateway to Hell."

I wasn't sure after that if he was unconscious or just ignoring me. His lidless eyes stared at the ceiling. I watched him breathe. I called Jason, but as usual, his voice mailbox was full, and I couldn't leave a message. That meant I would have to keep trying to actually catch him answering the phone. The doctor came in to see me about Jack, and we talked about skin grafts and costs. I assured him Jack had no insurance. The doctor decided to worry about that later. It would be touch and go for a while.

More go than touch. Later in the night, Edgar took me away to a hotel. The hospital called me there to let me know Jack had died.

I curled into a ball and shook with sobs while Edgar stroked my hair and shushed me.

———◆◆———

The Spider wanted us to spend a great deal on the funeral. Edgar and I decided that since we were paying for it, and since it was what we planned for ourselves, that cremation was the more economical alternative. Guilt shot out of the Spider's spinnerets, trying to catch one of us, but it couldn't find purchase. Egghead felt horrible and relieved at the same time, somewhat like I felt back when Frank died after a six-week stay in the hospital. Frank had been rotten to the core, and I was relieved when he was dead. I should have felt more that way about Jack, I suppose, but I could remember a Jack that Egghead couldn't.

I think Egghead hoped I'd make up with the Spider. I couldn't. Jack was the family scapegoat, and now that he was gone, Egghead thought everything was okay. I still saw the three of us as victims of horrible parents, and I could not forgive the Spider. This was a quarrel of its own, and that was pretty much it between me and Egghead and the Spider.

So Edgar and I returned to our lives, and if this were where the story ended, it would be another blip in the long saga of family dysfunction.

I can't forgive Frank. Egghead can't forgive Jack. Jack forgives all of us, maybe, including the man who might be in Hell. It looked like what Jack was doing was trying to live his faith. He could see the difference that embracing religion had made in him. Couldn't he take that message to his father?

I found myself visiting the rubble where God's Gift had been, embers and ash, the fire department making damned sure no gateway to Hell was still open. And yet, as I looked into the ruin, into the darkness, what I saw made me rethink everything. That night, I called Edgar, and told him I'd be home tomorrow, that it'd gotten too late, and I was going to get a room and be back in the morning.

I stopped by a local CVS and bought razor blades, and the rest you know. And no, before you ask, I wasn't trying to get to Frank. I was pretty sure nothing could change old Frank, and he'd stay in Hell anyway. I was trying to get to Jack, because I saw something in the darkness at God's Gift, a glimpse into Hell, a little boy sitting at the feet of our rapist, a little boy who had worn the shell of the adult he'd become at the end, but inside he was again an innocent. He'd been forgiven by God and his anger and madness had been swept away. He wanted that for his father.

My anger and madness are still here. I couldn't see Jack staying in Hell for Frank's sake, waiting for Frank to change. That's a lot like being beaten for cookies you didn't eat.

What? Will I try it again?

. . .

No. It was a moment. But these scars? I'm going to have to live with these scars for the rest of my life.

Witches is the third of the triptych I mentioned writing at Viable Paradise in 2009. This is the fantasy version of the prompt I was given. It was published in Spirit's Tincture *in 2016. It is an interesting examination of what it means to grow old.*

Witches

A heavy soldier's boot thudded against the cottage door. Mother Mabel, on her knees in front of the fireplace, craned her neck to see the wooden door burst open, rebound off the stone wall, and bounce close again. She caught glimpse of a broad soldier wearing smudgy, tarnished armor. Mabel creaked to her feet and shuffled across the swept dirt floor. She put her ear to it.

"Open up, in the name of the Witch King!"

Mabel frowned. The voice that fluttered on the other side of the door was more maid than mercenary. Maybe he'd had an accident in his youth.

"Who's there?" she said.

"Oh come on, Mabel," wheedled the feminine voice. "Open the door!"

Mabel had the reassurance of the Witch King that he would never, ever harm a seer. He valued the ability to prophecy the future. Crones in his kingdom were revered. The guard had been inexplicably rude.

She yanked the door open and glared at the man. "You! What do you want?"

A young beauty popped into view from behind the human sequoia with an inaudible ta-da!. Her pale hair was pulled up on high on her head in a centered ponytail that flopped freely as she struck her pose. Blue eyes sparkled. She wore a silver bikini that gleamed and twinkled, contrasting with the guard's hues of dirt and rust. The young woman waggled her fingers playfully. "Do you recognize me, Mabel?"

Mabel raised a hairy eyebrow worthy of a mountain man and scratched her chin. Hag whiskers tickled her fingers. "No."

"It's me, Mabel! It's Darcelinda!"

Now that Mabel was getting a better look, it appeared as though Darcelinda's armor had as much metal as the guard's helmet, spread more or less equally over key points of the body. She also wore metallic go-go boots and a gauzy turquoise cape that stopped shortly beneath her hips. Darcelinda giggled and twirled so Mabel could complete the picture.Not that Mabel wanted a complete picture.

"So," said Mabel. "Darcelinda."

"Yes!"

"You've lost weight," said Mabel flatly. "A lot of weight."

"Yes!" Her voice floated. "Isn't this wonderful? Look how young I am!"

Mabel sucked on her one good tooth as she considered. "You ought to be ashamed of yourself," she said. "Wearing armor like that, at your age!" She decisively began to shut the door.

"No, Mabel, wait!" Darcelinda grabbed the edge. "Wait here," she ordered the guard. She wriggled through the half open door into the cabin.

Dribbly candles littered Mabel's room, stuck to whatever surface could support them. On the floor in front of the fireplace was a dead crow, sliced open, inside of which Mabel had been scrying the future. Mabel eased herself into her rocking chair. "I don't take kindly to guards kicking on my door. I think it's against the law."

"Oh, I just wanted to show you my new command," said Darcelinda. "I say jump, he says how high. Actually, he says urgh, but he means how high."

"Darcelinda Wellbottom, I know you. You always leap before looking. That's what I say." Mabel rocked back in the chair. "I suppose the Witch King did this to you?"

Darcelinda leaned against the rough wall. "Yes! This is his beautification campaign. One incantation, and voila! An old hag is a nubile hag!" She preened. "Just think! No more rheumatism! No more hobbling around with aches and pains!"

"And no more seeing the future," said Mabel, rocking forward.

"Well, yes and no," waffled Darcelinda. "I can't *see* the future, but I know what my future is going to be. I'm in command of one of the Witch King's regiments now."

"That fellow outside? He's your regiment?"

Darcelinda drew herself up so that her cleavage was perpendicular to the wall. "Well, it's a start."

Mabel's head motioned toward the dead bird at the foot of the rocker. "You see that? Can you tell me what you see in there?"

Darcelinda crouched as best as she could in metal underwear and stirred the insides of the crow. "Spleen's a little...hey, is that spleen ruptured?"

"Tells me that someone's taking a journey." Mabel placed a gnarled hand on Darcelinda's smooth shoulder.

Darcelinda protested. "You mean me? No. Why, the Witch King respects all of us, remember? He wants to clean things up around here. And that's all. He's even traded in his black armor for something more pastel. It turns out that deep inside that shell of gloom the Witch King is a true altruist."

"I'm not changing," said Mabel. "Not if I have to wear an outfit that makes me look like a barbarian queen."

Darcelinda stamped a metallic boot. "You just had to rain on my parade, didn't you! You old faker! You've never been half the seer I was. And now you're jealous. Fine. Sit here and be old!"

Darcelinda stalked out the door, slamming it.

A short time after the dramatic exit, there was a tentative knocking. Mabel opened the door. The broad guard stood sheepishly, helmet rotating in his nervous hands. "Sorry about the kick, ma'am. It was orders."

"No harm done, sonny."

The big man shifted from foot to foot. "No change for you, then?"

"No boy, no change here."

"The Witch King hoped we could keep at least one. I guess you're it."

"All the others?" Mabel crossed her arms as the soldier nodded acquiescence. "Say," she said, studying the mental map she'd made of crow innards, "you're not the twisted entrails in the style of a knot, are you?"

"Ma'am?"

"The executioner, boy."

"Oh, no ma'am. The Witch King has trusted second lieutenants for that. I'm just a minion."

Mabel's head bobbed. "Just checking. Good night."

Door closed, candles lit, Mabel repositioned in her creaky rocker. She allowed herself the cup of tea she had hoped was in her future and rocked back and forth. Over the rim of her stoneware mug, she studied the dead crow and thought about the future.

Another piece for our animal shelter, Yellow Cat and the Man *was first published in* Indelible Companions. *Our cat Toby was quite the cat, and perhaps he embodies the title of this collection best. And it's only fitting that I cry my way out.*

Yellow Cat and the Man

Yellow Cat looked left, and then right, and then across the street. Across the street, The Man stood on the tip of a ladder, doing something to his porch. "This man understands me," said Yellow Cat. "He likes to climb things, like I do. We will be the best of friends." Yellow Cat padded across the street, all eagerness. It had been a while since he had been cuddled and tickled, and surely, surely The Man would cuddle and tickle him.

At first The Man seemed frustrated with him. "Get down from there!" Yellow Cat decided to amuse The Man with his high climbing prowess. "Come on! That's no place for you!" But then The Man smiled, and he went into his big house, and came out with The Woman. The Woman was also amused, but she seemed less so than the man. "You stinker!" said The Man.

"I think he's a stray," said The Woman.

Both The Man and The Woman couldn't see the difference between Yellow Cat and Peanut. Peanut was also a yellow cat, but he wasn't Yellow Cat. Peanut had a bushy tail and didn't like people. Yellow Cat had already decided to adopt The Man and The Woman. They figured out the difference one night when they saw them together outside. Some things had to be made obvious to The Man and The Woman.

The Man was easy. He worked outside more than The Woman. Yellow Cat liked his big yard with fluffy leaves to jump and play and pee in. The Man liked to hold Yellow Cat. When the weather became colder and ruffled Yellow Cat's fur, The Man would snuggle with Yellow Cat, and he even allowed Yellow Cat to climb inside The Man's coat. Oh, how Yellow Cat loved The Man's coat! So warm, and it smelled just like The Man, and eventually, a bit like Yellow Cat. It became scarred and pilled underneath Yellow Cat's claws, and The Woman would complain, but Yellow Cat didn't care, and he knew that The Man had too much good sense to care.

The Man built him a little house. This was good sense, as Yellow Cat planned on spending time on The Man's porch, and he needed somewhere to entertain, or at least to wait for his new Man and his new Woman to come home from that place they went to every day. At first, they seemed to want him to go back across the street. Foolish Man! Foolish Woman! Someone had to look after them now. He wasn't one to shirk his new responsibilities, not Yellow Cat.

Snow began to fall, but Yellow Cat was constant. His People needed him. He waited on the porch of The Man and The Woman's big house. From within, other cats hissed at him, but he wasn't one to shirk his new responsibilities, not Yellow Cat. The Woman was not easy, like the Man, but one night The Man came to Yellow Cat. Putting Yellow Cat inside his coat, The Man carved a hole for Yellow Cat in a new home, a large palace just for Yellow Cat, and The Woman smiled at Yellow Cat just a little more.

The Man was sometimes a little slow. Yellow Cat would bring him something to eat, and The Man didn't want it. He would go so far as to take things away from Yellow Cat.

"That's what cats do," said The Woman. The Woman was harder, but she understood Yellow Cat's motives. The Man took away rabbits, squirrels, and birds. Yellow Cat learned to eat first and hide food from The Man, but The Man must have had a good nose, because he almost always found the food. Stupid man!

Still, Yellow Cat loved The Man most of all. The Man bought him an outdoor swinging couch, and the two of them napped there in the summer and the spring and the fall. He called Yellow Cat nonsensical things, like Buddy Boo, and Turd, Stinker, and Mr. T, Toblerone, and King Tiger. The Woman did that too. The two of them would let him lie on his back and tickle his tummy. When he wanted them to stay, he would grab their hands with his paws, and they played well, and didn't mind the nicks. He protected them too. He chased all the stupid other cats out of the yard. One old white cat Yellow Cat chased out of the yard after The Man and The Woman had a stupid time of letting him stay, but he was old, so Yellow Cat went easy on him.

The Man came to see him every day. He told The Woman he had to polish the cat, and Yellow Cat would sit with The Man. These were the best times. The Man would let Yellow Cat into the crook of his arms, smashing his head as though he could love The Man more by smashing his head into him. Yellow Cat wanted The Man to know that he was the most important thing in the world to Yellow Cat, and that Yellow Cat took his responsibilities seriously, even if The Man wouldn't let Yellow Cat take proper care of him.

The Man adapted well for Yellow Cat. He bought a clawless paw and played with Yellow Cat. He gave Yellow Cat food every morning and every night and petted Yellow Cat. He poured water for Yellow Cat to drink every morning, even though in the cold weather it turned into a block of ice. The Man came to the cold garage in the winter and sat with Yellow Cat. He dug a path for Yellow Cat from the garage to the house in the coldest weather, so Yellow Cat's paw pads wouldn't be quite so cold. Yellow Cat loved The Man, and Yellow Cat knew The Man loved him.

The Woman would play games with Yellow Cat and The Man sometimes, and that was when Yellow Cat was happiest. Yellow Cat climbed from one set of their shoulders to the others, purring with glee. This was best in the cold garage on cold winter nights, because it was warm, and their coats were thick. They would pretend to talk for him in a high, squeaky voice. Yellow Cat felt that he was doing enough talking by purring, but they were his People, and he would humor them.

One might, Yellow Cat hurt his leg. He dragged himself home, and he waited for his people. He knew that they could make him feel better. The Woman was the one to hold him and sit with him, but The Man was always near, so near he could smell him. There were many days of pain and loneliness, but Yellow Cat knew his People would come for him. He worried about them a little, because it was so unlike The Man not to come.

Finally, The Man came, in his coat. The Woman came too. Yellow Cat climbed into The Man's coat, and all the pain and loneliness and fear were still there, but there was nothing that The Man and Yellow Cat couldn't last through together. When they were together, it was always the best of times, and Yellow Cat nestled into The Man, burrowed into him.

"I love you," said the Man. "You're my Buddy Boo."

Yellow Cat knew it was so. He purred to let The Man know that it was so. He was so happy his People had come, and he could look after them, finally, after worrying about them for so long. He closed his eyes, and they whispered to him, and stroked him for a long, long time. He started to clean himself, because he didn't want his People to see him messy, to show his People that they were his, and he would take care of them.

The Man and The Woman cuddled and petted Yellow Cat, and then Yellow Cat grew so very, very sleepy. He was happy though. He was with his people again, on The Woman's lap, and The Man stroking him, and everything smelling like The Man. "Shhh," said The Man. "You'll be all better soon. Visit me in my dreams."

The Man was right. Yellow Cat went into a deep, peaceful sleep on the outdoor swinging couch, the wind ruffling and kissing his fur. Every night, just as The Man went to sleep, he would wait there so The Man could polish the cat. After all, The Man was his, and Yellow Cat wasn't one to shirk his responsibilities.

Afterword

Unlike my last collection of short stories, this collection has loss as a through line. Not that every story is depressing or sad, but I think mortality is a place I have become stuck in as a writer. Another factor these stories have in common is most of them have been published by other people first, so it took a while to get them into a self-published collection.

Each of these stories has many people to thank for reading and advice. They were also written some 10-13 years ago, so I know I'd forget someone if I started listing names. Therefore, it's probably best for me to thank everyone, and if you think you're being thanked, you're probably right.

These days, my time is largely taken up with writing novels and serials. I am currently working on the middle grade series *Abigail Rath Versus* and the Gothic series, *The Klaereon Scroll*. I'm also writing *The Autumn Warrior and the Ice Sword* over at Kindle Vella. All this is to say I doubt that there will be another collection of shorts for a few more years, although I already have two stories that most likely will find their way into it. And only one of them is about mortality, so maybe I'm coming out of it.

I hope these stories give you something to think about. If you're interested in more of my writing, I'd recommend you check out my website cathschaffstump.com

--Catherine Schaff-Stump
July 13, 2021

About the Author

Cath Schaff-Stump writes fantasy for children and adults. She writes funny stories, dark stories, and everything in between. She is the author of the Klaereon Scroll series and the Abigail Rath Versus series. Cath lives and works in Iowa. During the day, she teaches English at a local community college. More of her fiction has been published by Paper Golem Press, Daydreams Dandelion Press, and in *The Mammoth Book of Dieselpunk*. You can find her online at Facebook, Goodreads, Amazon, @cathschaffstump, and cathschaffstump.com. Follow Cath's Kindle Vella serial *The Autumn Warrior and the Ice Sword*.

* 9 7 9 8 7 7 7 4 2 4 0 7 5 *